# A MAIL ORDER BRIDE FOR THE BOUNTY HUNTER

## WESTERN BRIDES

## BLYTHE CARVER

## 1

———

Brenda Watson stared at her reflection in the mirror, taking in her long, wavy, nearly-black hair and bright, interested green eyes. She wished she didn't have to put her hair up. She liked to keep it down and did so as often as she could.

It was a terrible day, as far as she was concerned. To her father, it was a day to remember. This morning at breakfast, he'd informed her with no flourish that he'd come to a decision with Mr. Alfred Lawler. She was to marry his son, Micah, whom she'd gone to the academy of higher learning with for one year on a special scholarship for women. She was one of only two women in the college for that year. It had been her goal since winning the scholarship to open the eyes of modern men and bring them into the future—a future that accepted women on the same level as it accepted men. Society shouldn't just be a place for the advancement of men.

Brenda was determined to make that opinion known. She had a brilliant, sharp mind and wasn't afraid to use it.

Unfortunately, she was also plagued with the insatiable desire not to disrespect her family. It didn't help that Micah was her friend, and she knew for a fact that he was in love with a young lady named Lydia.

She would have to talk to him at the dinner party. She already had an idea forming in her mind.

BRENDA SNUCK around the rose bush, peeking into the large dining hall. She searched for Micah among the throng of guests that had shown up. She hated to disappoint them and betray her father, but she thought it was best to disappear before he made the announcement and embarrassed himself in front of all his distinguished guests.

She didn't want to hurt her father. Ever since her

mother died three years ago, he had tried his best to understand his growing daughter. She was twenty now, and he was determined to marry her to Micah's family because Alfred was one of his best friends. They'd joked when the two were young how nice it would be if the two fell in love and got married, making them related through marriage.

Now the time had come, but Micah and Brenda's feelings had never gotten stronger than a friendship.

She finally saw him and waved at him frantically, trying to get his attention. His eyes were scanning the room, a distinct look of boredom on his face. When his eyes flicked to her, his expression lit up. Brenda thought how happy their fathers would have been if that had been a look of love.

It was, in a way, but not the way their fathers wanted.

Now when he looked around, it was with suspicion. He made sure no one was paying attention to him and slipped down the hallway. He came out a side door typically used by the house staff.

"Micah," she said, a surprising sense of relief washing over her. "I'm so glad you saw me. Dinner is about to start. I want you to talk to our fathers. I have made up my mind. I'm not going to put either one of us through this. I know you want to marry Lydia.

The only way I can free you up to do that is if I leave town for a while."

Micah looked distraught, his eyebrows furrowing. "Oh no, Brenda. I don't want you to have to leave. This is your home. That's not fair to you at all."

Affection for her friend filled her heart. She gave him a warm smile. "You are such a good man. Lydia is so lucky. But I've made up my mind, Micah. It won't be changed."

"But where will you go? What will you do?"

"I have a friend in Low Branch. I know he and his new wife will let me stay for a while. I think a few months' space will help our fathers see they've made a rash decision that isn't going to make their children happy. They aren't thinking about that right now, I'm sure of it. Have you told your father you don't want to marry me?"

"I did. He said it was ridiculous and that you and I get along wonderfully. I couldn't deny that, but I told him we aren't more than friends." He raised an eyebrow. "What do you think? Can you force it?"

Brenda giggled, recognizing his humor. "I don't want to force it. And what about Lydia? I couldn't live my life knowing I'd taken away the dreams of two people because I didn't stand up to my father. I love you, Micah. But not like that. You know that."

He nodded. "I know. I feel the same way about you. I only want the best for you. I want you to be as happy as you could ever be. Just not with me."

They both laughed at that.

"Are you planning on leaving right now?" Micah asked. "What was the plan you had in mind. I'm sure you thought one up. It would be very unlike you not to think of a solution to the problem you're confronted with."

Brenda was flattered by the compliment. She grinned at him. "The ticket is waiting at the train station. I notified my friend, Jeremiah, through telegram this morning after my father told me what he was going to announce and what the real reason for this dinner party was, and they are waiting for me this evening. I am leaving in a few minutes. Please tell my father in half an hour after my train leaves. It will be before the announcement. If you see him getting ready to announce it, stop him."

"They aren't going to eat the entire dinner without you. I doubt they will even start without you."

"I'm leaving now. My train takes off at fifteen

after six. If you can tell him after or around them, that would be best."

Micah pulled out his pocket watch and flipped it open. He nodded at her.

"Okay. And Brenda..." He gave her a quick hug, whispering, "be careful," in her ear.

2

—————

A month had passed since Brenda came to Low Branch, a month that passed with so much going on it seemed like hardly any time at all. As soon as she arrived, she and Jeremiah reunited with the same close kinship they'd shared when they were young and spent more time together during summer vacations and holidays.

He offered to put her in a cottage on the outskirts of Low Branch where she could plant a garden, have some chickens, grow some vegetables and do anything she wanted with it. She begged him not to bestow such a grand gift on her, but he said he'd gotten a windfall and could afford it. Besides, he'd said, the cottage was on some land he was getting ready to purchase and was going to rent out anyway.

She'd taken the gift and made it her own. Just afterward, they all found out just how much Jeremiah's mother, Clarice, wanted the cottage for herself. She began to spread vicious rumors about Brenda, saying she would end up a spinster because of her bad attitude and gold-digging ways. She said Brenda was waiting for the man with the most money to come along.

These were some of the mild rumors Clarice spread about Brenda. It hurt her to think the older woman would stoop to such measures, destroying her reputation with people she barely knew before she had a chance to establish herself with them and show them who she really was.

Much to Brenda's chagrin, Clarice had made things so difficult for Jeremiah and his wife, Isabelle, he had told her to find somewhere else to live. He'd escorted her to the buggy he'd commissioned to take her to her sister's place twenty minutes away.

"This looks so beautiful, Isabelle," Brenda said, setting a flowerpot down on the lowest shelf in front of her. It fit perfectly, but there wasn't much room for it to grow. She changed her mind and moved it to one of the upper shelves where it would have more room.

The sun shining through the other side of the

window would give each plant the same amount of light throughout the day. She had bunched together the ones that needed the same amount so they would hopefully grow at a consistent rate with one another.

"Thank you for your help, Brenda. I don't know what I'd do without your help."

Brenda laughed softly. "I've been here a month. You had this place looking great long before I got here. Anyway, I've been thinking about what we were talking about yesterday. I think you might be right. I do want to get married. I don't have any prospects. I've been writing to Micah, and he says my father is still adamant about marrying me off, even though he knows I have no suitors at all."

"Micah has settled that, though, hasn't he?" Isabelle asked, her eyes focused on the plant in front of her as she clipped the dead leaves away. She glanced at Brenda. "He's such a nice young man. It truly is a shame you two didn't fall in love with each other. You would have been a perfect couple from what you've said about him."

Brenda maintained her smile, running her eyes over the shelves of plants she'd just put together. There was one hole to fill.

"It's true. We are the best of friends. He's one of

the reasons I wish I didn't have to leave Frontier. If it wasn't for him, I wouldn't know what was going on except through the angry letters from my father. It's because of Micah I'm able to respond to my father with kindness." She felt a twinge of regret that she'd had to flee her hometown in the first place.

"I know you love your father," Isabelle said, drawing Brenda's attention away from the shelves of plants. "I can tell every time you talk about him. The letters from Micah have been a great relief to you. I've noticed that, too. You've read both of their letters to me. I can see it."

Brenda turned away from her work, strolling over to a bench Isabelle had placed in the middle of the greenhouse so she could get off her feet whenever she wanted to. The origin of that idea, she'd told Brenda, was when she was eight months pregnant and still wanting to work in there. She had to sit down every ten minutes, it seemed, but at least she'd been able to keep doing what she loved to do. Plus, she liked having her own money from the restoration of tired, dying plants for her friends and neighbors to selling fresh treasures to new lovers of all things green and growing.

"I love being here with you, though, Isabelle," she said comfortably, sitting back on the bench against the railing behind her. "I'm so grateful for you giving me this job and Jeremiah letting me have that cottage. I will never be able to pay you back."

"You don't have to, and you know it. I know you feel some obligation, though. You just keep being my friend, and we'll be just fine."

Brenda nodded. Jeremiah and Isabelle had made her feel more welcome than she'd felt in her own hometown. The big parties her father and brothers threw weren't meant to include her. That's why she hadn't thought twice about the dinner party of her father's until he'd told her that morning what his plan was.

It was a good thing she'd already been making her plans to get out before that could happen.

Even at those lavish parties, Brenda didn't feel actually welcome. They were in her own home, and she still didn't feel welcome.

It wasn't that Brenda didn't want to find a husband. She enjoyed being able to make her own decisions, but that didn't mean she wanted to be a spinster. She wanted to marry. When she found a husband to love, a man who would give her children to cherish and raise with his help.

So far, Brenda had stayed to herself. She wanted to get to know the people in town before she put herself out there for a suitor. It didn't help that Clarice had put a damper on things, forcing her to go on the offensive and prove she was not the woman Clarice made her out to be. It wasn't easy because Clarice actually had friends in the small town. People knew her.

They didn't know Brenda and judged her before she even got there.

It wasn't fair, but Brenda had already learned that making a change was up to her.

3
_____________

The bartender looked up when Hendricks Potter walked in. It was typical, even though Hendricks hadn't been in the saloon before. He was tall, 6 foot 5 to be exact, with broad shoulders and muscles that intimidated the majority of men.

He'd been blessed, in his opinion, with a personality that was much less intimidating. He was smart—but not too smart—and funny—but not as funny as he wished he could be. Having a good personality was important to him, and it wasn't for the usual reasons.

Hendricks was twenty-nine years old and had been working as a bounty hunter since he was eighteen. He was one of the youngest he knew of and had still been doing the job longer than some of the other older men. More than a decade was quite a lot of experience.

He was good at his job, too, and enjoyed it. Both facts made it easier for him to do his job.

"Hendricks Potter," he introduced himself to the bartender, holding out his hand. In all his years on the job, Hendricks had trained himself to make a quick judgment about a man by shaking his hand upon greeting. With men he knew, he could detect what mood they were in by how tight or loose their grip was.

In strangers, he was given a baseline in the hopes that those he met meant him no harm when they first met. So far, his strategy had worked in his favor.

"Douglas Raintree," the man replied, taking his hand. "Call me Doug. This here's my saloon. Glad ya stumbled in. Ya stayin' for a while?"

"In here, maybe. In this town, probably not. I don't know yet. We'll just have to wait and see how things pan out."

"Well, glad ta have ya here fer now. What can I get ya? Beer?"

"That would be great, thanks. Listen, I'm lookin' for a man. You think you can help?"

Doug studied his face. Hendricks did the same,

wondering what the man thought of him. He tried to look amiable. Hendricks figured he was sizing him up, trying to decide what Hendricks would do if he said no.

Hendricks was aware that many men told him whatever they knew—honest or not—just because they were afraid he would beat them up. He'd rarely used his fists on anyone other than an outlaw, a violent prisoner.

He slid onto one of the stools, and Doug provided a beer for him, sliding the thick mug over to him across the counter. "You look tired," the man said.

Hendricks nodded. "Yeah, I'm pretty tuckered out. I been lookin' for a man for three weeks. Me and my partner, Denver, split up to try to track this feller down." He fished in his back pocket and pulled out a doubled-folded paper from it. Using one hand, he unfolded it and pressed down on the four pieces with his fingers to flatten it as much as he could. "This feller. You know him? Seen him anywhere around here?"

Doug looked at the poster, focusing on it for a good, long moment. Hendricks was gratified the bartender didn't just dismiss him outright. "Can't say as I've seen him, but that don't mean nothing. He'd have to come up here and get a beer. He come in with anyone else, I wouldn't see him. I live upstairs and don't go out much, so," He slid the poster back to Doug. "Can't say as I've seen 'im. I'll tell ya, though, ya can hang around and look for him or ask anyone in town. Most people are friendly here in Horsepasture. If they've seen anybody suspicious around here, they'll tell ya."

"Thanks, Doug," Hendricks replied, lifting his glass up. "I appreciate that." He took a long swig, enjoying the taste as it slid over his tongue. Some beer was better than others, he thought. He swiveled around on the stool and let his eyes roam over the crowd. It was fairly full. He was impressed. Horsepasture was a very small town, and it seemed everyone had come to the bar.

He glanced back at Doug, who was leaning over the bar, both arms crossed in front of him. "It usually this packed in your saloon?" he asked over the hum of voices.

Doug nodded several times, shrugging. "It is on a Friday. We got a big weekend planned. People gatherin' in here to talk about it."

Hendricks was interested in the town's weekend plans. He turned back around.

"What's going on?"

"Supposed to be a wedding. Carlson boy and Weedle girl. They been courting for a while now."

Hendricks lifted his eyebrows curiously. "Odd way to say it, though," he remarked. "Supposed to be? Does that mean it might not happen?"

"Well, there's been some talk around town that the boy might be backing out. He's a good kid, and there ain't nothin' wrong with her. But then there's good ol' Barty, and he's been tryin' for that girl's affections since they was just kids. So now we ain't sure if sweet little Jo is gonna follow through with it all. She's..." Doug gave him a look of regret. "Well, she's a bit wishy-washy, if ya ask me. Sweet girl, don't get me wrong. Wouldn't want to get on the wrong side of that family. I'm just speakin' my mind, ya know, because you're a stranger, and you ain't invested in either family."

Hendricks had to admit that was true. He nodded at the man. "I understand."

"Ya know, you might spot that man yer lookin' fer if ya stick around tonight. If he's in Horsepasture, he'll be bound to show his face in here. Everybody will come and go tonight. Exceptin' the kids, ya know."

Hendricks nodded. "Yeah, okay. I think I will. Thanks, Doug. I appreciate the invitation."

"You got it, Hendricks."

He turned around once again and looked out over the crowd. This was Denver's kind of scene. His partner was a personable man, older and just stuffed to the brim with charisma. He had a way with women but would never be in a relationship with one. He'd lost his one true love when he was young and hadn't found another woman who could capture his heart and take it from the one who was gone. She wouldn't come back. She had passed from influenza and was buried six feet under.

Hendricks had been there for the whole thing. Denver was older than him by a few years. He'd been in love with Diana when he first met Hendricks and offered to partner up with him, teach him the tricks of the trade. He'd been there for Denver while Diana was suffering and when she died, as well. His friend was very important to him.

Splitting up wasn't something the two men usually did, but they'd been forced to when Kelsey Bradshaw, the man he was after, had vanished from the last small town they knew he'd been to. There were two trails the outlaw would likely follow. One went toward Richmond, a nearby larger city, and the other went to Low Branch, a smaller Texas town. They'd drawn straws, and Hendricks had gotten the smaller of the two, meaning he would go to the smaller town. The reason it was the short straw was that Kelsey was less likely to go to a larger city.

The outlaw was notorious for choosing the narrow, rocky path that led to the smaller cities and towns. Hendricks was always willing to be the one in pursuit. This time was no different.

Just as Doug predicted, the saloon got rowdy around dinnertime and stayed buzzing most of the night. It was pulling into nine o'clock when Hendricks decided it was time to get a room at the hotel for the night. A good sleep would restore his mind and his faith.

Hendricks paid his tab and slid off the barstool. He turned toward the door and what he saw made him stumble a little. He fell forward and hit a man standing near him. The effect of the hit forced the drink from the man's hand, and it splashed onto the man in front of him.

This ripple effect made the saloon turn into chaos.

"I'm sorry," Hendricks said to the man he'd bumped into. The man turned around, and though he was smaller—like most men—a certain look glazed over his eyes, and Hendricks knew what was coming next.

Hendricks wasn't just six-five and built like a brick house. He also had jet-black hair and green eyes that made most men see green before they knew what kind of man he was. They wanted to fight him, not just to prove their manhood but also in an attempt to *mess up his pretty face*, which was a phrase he'd heard too many times to count and hated more than words could express.

He saw that look come over the drunken man's eyes and prepared himself. He had to think quickly because he knew a fight was inevitable. Knowing his own strength, Hendricks normally did everything he could to avoid a physical fight. This time was no exception.

The man spun on him. Knowing what was coming next from pure experience, Hendricks ducked at the perfect time. It wasn't perfect, however, for the man who had come up behind Hendricks. He was clocked right in the jaw and knocked into the bar.

Hendricks's eyes widened. He didn't come back up. He immediately moved, crouching, through the sea of bodies to try to get to the front of the saloon.

It was Kelsey he'd seen. He was almost sure of it.

That's why he'd stumbled. And it seemed to him like the outlaw was looking him directly in the eyes. That wasn't lucky for him. Kelsey was aware they were following him and had threatened the bounty hunters on more than one occasion, taunting them and laughing when they didn't catch him.

It was infuriating.

The two men, however, had gone after worse criminals who got away numerous times before they were caught. That was it, though. They *were* caught. He and Denver always got their man. They had a one hundred percent success rate so far.

The number of men fighting each other seemed to grow until everyone in the bar was fighting. Hendricks searched, sure he saw Kelsey somewhere in the saloon. If he was fighting someone else, it would be impossible to spot him among the rest of them.

Hendricks was surprisingly stealthy for being such a big man. He got down as far as he could and moved around the people in the saloon, even past the shapely legs of a saloon girl, who was pulling on the arms of a man and begging him not to fight anymore.

Hendricks was nearly to the door when he finally saw the man he was pursuing. Just as he'd thought, Kelsey was standing to the side, watching the action through narrow eyes, a sneer on his lips. Hendricks still didn't know if he'd seen him or not. Surely if he'd seen Hendricks, Kelsey would have hightailed it out of there right away.

Or maybe he just wasn't afraid of being caught. He probably thought he would always get away. Hendricks felt like pouncing across the room. He would have, in fact, if a large body hadn't gotten between the two of them, wrestling with someone else.

Kelsey turned his head, watching the two men as they fought. His eyes moved past them, and he caught sight of Hendricks. This time, there was no doubt the outlaw saw him.

Hendricks stood up straight, bulging his chest out and balling up his fists. His jaw set, he prepared to stomp toward the outlaw, shoving the fighting men out of the way if he had to.

Before he could do what he was thinking, Kelsey, who was a thinner, wiry man, moved so quickly Hendricks almost lost sight of him. Instead of darting for the front door, which was closest to both men, Kelsey ran into the thick of the action. Hendricks growled, unhappy with the outlaw's decision. Unlike Kelsey, Hendricks wasn't able to maneuver through a tight crowd of people in a fairly small room like they were in. The only way he could get through was by throwing people out of his way. That was possible but usually caused a lot more trouble and damage than he cared for. Plus, he would be blamed, and he didn't want that either.

Hendricks risked getting punched and pulled into the fighting by going through the chaos. He kept low, ducking and twisting so he could sort of roll through them instead of joining them in the fray.

There had to be a back door. Most saloons— shoot, most buildings had back doors. That had to be where Kelsey was going. He wasn't the type to stay and fight. He would rather flee.

As he passed the counter, heading for the door to the back room where the door had to be, he caught sight of Doug, who was leaping up on the counter of his bar with a shotgun. The next moment, he fired it straight into his ceiling, creating a massive hole that let in light as debris from the broken ceiling and roof fell to the floor.

Doug roared in outrage, shrieking for the fighting to stop. It did, and an instant quiet fell over the room. Hendricks went through the door and found himself in a back kitchen. The stove was hot, a pot of stew bubbling, letting off a delicious scent.

He thought about how hungry he was and how much he wished he could stay for just one bowl of that beef stew as he rushed to the back door, which was still swinging open slightly from Kelsey just going through. Hendricks hadn't seen him go through, but he was sure that's where the outlaw had gone.

It had grown dark. He stepped out into the night, hearing a scuffling noise to his left. It was Kelsey, grabbing a horse that probably wasn't his.

"Stay right there," Hendricks yelled out, knowing the outlaw wasn't about to stop for him. He yanked his gun from the holster, but he couldn't see well enough to actually aim and shoot. In a frantic motion, he jumped down the three steps to the ground, ran around the side of the building to get to his horse, and pulled himself up in the saddle in one sweeping motion.

**4**

———

"What do you think?" Brenda asked Isabelle, showing her a sketch she'd made of herself, Isabelle, and Jeremiah. They were standing in the picture, talking amongst the trees outside the community hall in the town square.

"It's an exact replica of the three of us," Isabelle gushed, smiling wide. "I love it. Thank you. Can I keep it?"

"Yes, of course."

"I can't wait to show it to Jeremiah. He will love it." She eyed the sketch, holding it in front of her with both hands.

Her complimentary behavior made Brenda feel good. Isabelle had come over for lunch and to do some crafts with Brenda. She'd brought over some ribbon and beads so they could make bracelets for the girls at the church and beaded pendants and pins for the boys.

"Oh." Brenda suddenly remembered why she'd been so excited for Isabelle to come over for their lunch date. She shot up from her chair and rushed over to the small table by the back door that led out to the garden. "I got a letter from Micah."

"How exciting. Does he say anything interesting?"

Brenda chuckled. "Micah is always interesting. And this letter is actually not one of the more pleasant ones. It seems my father has been talking to his father about everything and is still very unhappy with me. He has a scheme in mind, I think. At least that's what Micah is implying."

She pulled the two-page letter from the envelope and handed it to her.

Isabelle gave her a curious look. "You just want me to go ahead and read it?"

"I want to see if you have the same thoughts as me."

Isabelle's thin eyebrows lifted. "About what?"

"Whether my father is still angry and if his new scheme is something I should be worried about. I'll be very honest with you, Bellie. I wouldn't have been surprised if he tried to spread harmful rumors about Lydia the way Clarice did about me."

Isabelle chuckled, unfolding the papers and holding them open as she ran her eyes over the words. "Not by blood, they aren't," she murmured. Brenda could tell she was reading the letter. There was nothing about it that was private to Brenda. Micah was a very open communicator and spoke with a bluntness she'd gotten used to long ago. It was one of the traits they shared and equally appreciated about each other.

"Ah," Isabelle mumbled, nodding. "I see what you're talking about. But the only way he can do this is if you're there. You aren't there. He'd need your cooperation for everything he's been talking about."

Brenda nodded back. She'd been thinking the same thing. "I don't want to go back. I want to find the man I'm going to marry on my own. I don't want his help. He's not thinking about my happiness. He's thinking about the best business deal he can make."

Isabelle tilted her head to the side and gave Brenda a warm, friendly look. "You know, it really surprises me."

"What does?" Brenda asked, leaning on the table with her arms.

"Since you've come here, you've talked about your father in such... odd ways. It's unmistakable that you love him. He must have raised you with plenty of love, or you would be resentful of him. You would speak ill of him. But you simply want to make up your own mind, and he won't let you. I think you're right. He's using you like a commodity. That's a shame. But it doesn't mean he doesn't love you, and it's obvious that's your view of thinking here, isn't it?"

Brenda grinned. "That sounds like a really long way of asking me if I love my pa. My answer to that is of course. I love him. I know he's only doing this because he thinks it's the right thing for me. He's looking at it from a business point of view. Of course he is. But he still loves me. I know he does. I can't speak badly of him. I left quietly because I didn't want a confrontation with him."

"Aren't you afraid of what he thinks about you for leaving? He seems too upset. It must feel awful to know he is not being reasonable about this very important matter."

Brenda nodded. Isabelle was such an understanding person. She was glad to have such a good friend to vent to and get advice from.

"I really am. Well, perhaps not *afraid* of what

he'll think and say. He's never hurt me. He's never laid a hand on me in punishment or for any reason at all." Brenda gave a start, realizing her father hugged her about twice a year. Her birthday and Christmas morning. Otherwise, there was no touching whatsoever. They were rarely in the same room most of the time. "I'm only worried because I regret having to do this. I wish he had let me make up my own mind without forcing my hand. I miss my home." She laughed abruptly, which brought a confused look to Isabelle's slender face. "I'm laughing because that's not true either. Not really. I love the cottage. I don't ever want to leave it. I might be a spinster for life, just so I never have to leave this place."

She looked around the small living room they were in. It was decorated just the way she wanted. It was a work in progress, as she still had room for more trinkets, decorations, and pictures to hang on the wall.

"Maybe I'll frame this and put it up," she said, pulling a sketch she'd created toward her.

Isabelle handed the letter back over, having read through it quickly. "I think you have to address this before your father does something he regrets. Like spread rumors about your friend's sweetheart. That's going to hurt a lot of innocent people."

Brenda nodded. "That's what I was thinking. And I was also thinking about the way you and Jeremiah got together. You two are so perfect for each other. I know you got together through one of the marriage magazines or an ad for marriage. I want to do that, too. I think it's the perfect way to settle this."

Brenda studied her friend's face, but it was impossible to tell what Isabelle was thinking by what she saw. She looked thoughtful, but that was it. After a few moments of thinking, Isabelle replied.

"If that's what you want to do, Brenda, you know I'm all on board with you. I'll do anything I can to help you do what makes you happy."

She was glad she wasn't alone in her venture. "I never thought about it before. But seeing the way you and Jeremiah are together, I can't help but hope I can find the same kind of happiness you two have. I'm going to try to go to him, though, wherever he is, because with the way people talk about me here in Low Branch, I'm afraid he will hear horrible things about me if he comes here."

"Oh, Brenda. I haven't heard anyone say anything bad about you."

"No one stood up for me when Clarice was spreading her lies."

Isabelle gave her a sympathetic look. "Clarice knows everyone, and no one knows you. Jeremiah spoke up for you. He swayed many people back toward you. The townsfolk don't all hate you, my dear. They really don't."

Brenda gave her a smile but couldn't help thinking she didn't believe it.

## 5

Hendricks rode through the woods after Kelsey as fast as he could. The path was clear enough. It was the lack of light that was his problem. The horse wasn't about to run into a tree.

He was using the light ahead of him coming from the lantern Kelsey was carrying. He had no idea if the outlaw knew he was behind him. He was nervous and apprehensive about what he was running into. He wished Denver was there. Two against one made things so much easier.

Hendricks could see a glow in the sky not far in the distance. He recognized it as firelight. Kelsey was going toward a campsite. Was he meeting other men? Was Hendricks riding into an ambush?

He slowed his horse, deciding to go forward but with caution. He was a bounty hunter. It wasn't his job to run away when the odds didn't look good. But he didn't have to run recklessly into the fight either.

Hendricks pulled back, keeping his eye on the glowing sky. He got off the beaten trail and slid out of the saddle when he could actually see the haphazard ring of large rocks with a blazing fire within the circle. There were two men sitting facing it.

Hendricks left his horse with the reins thrown around a low-hanging branch and crept slowly toward the campsite. He watched Kelsey ride up to the campsite.

"Hey, hey, hey," one of the men said, standing awkwardly, leaning all his weight on one leg. "Who goes there, friend or foe?"

Kelsey chuckled without humor, walking toward the fire. "It's me, you fool. You know who I am."

"Right," the man said, shifting his weight and then dropping to the stump he'd been sitting on. "Foe. Shoulda known."

"Leave it, Mutt," the third man said just before putting the piece of dried meat between his teeth and ripping off the end roughly. He chewed so hard even Hendricks could feel how tough the meat must have been. He spoke through the chews, his words distorted as a result. He didn't look at Kelsey, who walked casually to the fire, reached to the plate by the one called Mutt, and took a piece of jerky from it. He shook the meat in Mutt's direction, a sneer on his face. "He ain't a foe. He ain't a friend, neither. He's just Bradshaw, the worst outlaw in town." He chuckled, still facing the fire, swallowing his food and ripping off another piece with his strong teeth.

Kelsey dropped to a fallen tree log that had been pulled to the firepit as a chair. "I hear ya sarcasm, Buddy, and I'm not sure I appreciate it."

Hendricks didn't think he sounded like it bothered him all that much. He searched his mind for information about outlaws named Mutt and Buddy. Nothing came to mind. He went own on one knee, peering through the leaves at the men. It would do him no good to run up on them and try to take them in. He wasn't capable of anything like that alone. He valued the idea of living to fight another day.

He wasn't known for being reckless.

With that thought in mind, he pushed away from the men, who had fallen quiet. He ran through a few scenarios in his mind as he crept silently back to his horse. He lifted one hand and put it on the reins to remove them from the limb when he felt something poke him in the side. He didn't need to feel it twice to know what it was.

He spun around, swinging. His fist slammed into the side of the head of a man almost as tall as him but not nearly as broad. Unfortunately, his girth made him an easy target, and he felt a bullet slide through his skin.

Aware that it was only a flesh wound that would probably bleed more than anything else, he put his full weight into the man, determined to squash him before he could shoot again. The sound of the shot was enough to alert the men at the campfire, and Hendricks wasn't in the mood to get in a fight with three other men.

He was losing blood faster than he would have liked. He only knew because he could feel it dripping down his side, and the strange sensation of fatigue began to take him over.

He pulled himself up into the saddle and jerked on the reins.

"You followed me," Kelsey shrieked. "You gonna get what you came for, bounty hunter."

Hendricks clenched his jaw, his heart pounding hard in his chest. He leaned back as he pulled the horse to the left. He kicked the animal's flanks and held on. He reached back to his saddle bags, which he typically kept light so as to save the horse's strength.

He yanked the towel from the left one and shoved it into his shirt, tearing the buttons off in the process. It burned when he pressed the fabric against the wound. It would need to be cleaned as soon as possible, or he would get an infection. For now, all he needed to do was get to safety. He'd gotten a hotel room in Horsepasture, but now he couldn't go back. Not unless he got away from Kelsey and the rest of the gang.

"Where are you, Denver?" he murmured, fighting against the pain and concentrating on where he was going. He was going into the darkness, and that wasn't good. He would have to rely on the horse knowing where he was going.

Several bullets whizzed past his head, but it was probably too dark for any of those men to aim perfectly. He was grateful for that, at least. He ducked and kept low.

Where was the nearest town?

His eyes adjusted to the darkness, and he thanked God the moon was nearly full, and there wasn't a cloud in the sky. Hendricks's eyes were closing. He felt so weak. He needed to rest. He couldn't let himself, though, or he might fall off the horse. He was stronger than most men. He reminded himself of that repeatedly as he pushed on.

Hendricks pulled in a deep breath and sat up straight in the saddle. He fought for consciousness, pressing the towel into the wound harder, determined to stop the bleeding as much as he could. It was bleeding profusely for a flesh wound. Maybe it was deeper than he thought.

There was something up ahead. A barn, he thought. Or a house. Too small to be a house, he told himself. Had to be a barn.

He gently pulled the reins to the left so the horse would turn toward the barn. As he got closer, he could see one side of the roof had caved in. It was definitely not being used. If there was a house nearby, it was probably not being used either.

But he wasn't going to make it to the house if there was one. He had to stop. He had to lay his head down.

**6**

———

Despite Isabelle's reassurance that "everyone didn't hate her," Brenda still felt their eyes boring into her wherever she went. She tried to ignore it but couldn't help noticing when they avoided talking to her, walking right past her without even acknowledging her existence.

Brenda felt foolish being so self-conscious about it, but she'd only just arrived when Clarice decided to badmouth her. She wasn't expecting it and had no way to combat it. She wasn't vindictive. She didn't want to take revenge. She just wished it hadn't happened to begin with.

She stepped into the Postmaster's and went

quickly to the counter, giving Paul an anxious look. "Do I have anything today?" she asked politely.

It was the first time the man had ever smiled at her, and she was surprised by how gracious and warm it looked.

"As a matter of fact, you do, Miss Brenda. You got a letter. And here it is." As he spoke, Paul twisted his upper body and retrieved a letter from a slot behind him. "Came just this mornin' it did. Thinkin' of goin' home already?"

Brenda wasn't expecting a conversation. The man had never initiated one before. She smiled at him, as friendly as she could manage. "I'm not going home. Is it from my father?" The idea that he had written to her made her a little sick to her stomach. She glanced down at the envelope and saw the return address read *Lancer, Texas.*

"Oh, it's from Lancer," she remarked, knowing who it was from. It was the man she'd written to, Leonard Franklin. She was excited he'd written back to her. Lancer was only a two-hour drive. She wouldn't be far from her friend and his wife, who made her feel more like family than her own father, at that point. She wouldn't be far from him either, though, and that was as it should be. Someday they would reconcile. She had no doubt. She gave the man a new grin. "I'm not from Lancer. This is just a friend. Thank you so much. I appreciate it."

"Anytime, dear, anytime."

Brenda waved at him as she walked to the entrance and left the small brown building. She hurried down the street, her eyes on the letter. She didn't pay attention to anyone around her as she strolled quickly to Isabelle's flower shop.

A bell over her head tinkled when Brenda entered, a sound that was etched in her memory and she would associate with Isabelle for the rest of her life. It was pleasant and sent a warmth through her she enjoyed very much.

"Isabelle," she exclaimed at the counter where her friend was just seconds later. She knew she had to be oozing excitement. "I got a letter. I got a letter. Oh, this is so exciting." She giggled a little, covering her mouth with her hand.

"Open it up. Let's see what it says." Isabelle shared her exuberance, coming around the counter and hovering over her shoulder, her eyes anxious.

"Okay, here I go." Brenda didn't intentionally make her friend or herself wait. She was just terrified. It was the first one. Was it wise not to wait for any others? Who said she wouldn't? Her thoughts raced through her mind as she turned the envelope over and slid the opener her friend gave her through it.

She withdrew the paper. It was tri-folded. She opened it up, revealing what she considered to be quite elegant writing. The author was a creative man, she thought.

"He requests another letter from me," she said, feeling a bit put off by the tone of the letter. She wasn't about to tell Isabelle that, especially since she'd found her own husband that way and Brenda's friend couldn't be a happier man.

Isabelle, however, was not a stupid woman and caught on to the gist of Brenda's words and the meaning behind the tone. "You don't sound pleased," she said.

Isabelle took in the short note, the abruptness of the letter. Perhaps she was being too judgmental. He might be a shy man without much to say when writing. He might be a man who is much better at speaking than writing letters. She cleared her throat, looking up at Isabelle while taking in a deep breath.

"It's not that I'm not pleased. I guess I just, I'm just nervous. I don't know this man, and the whole point of me writing to him was to go there and get to know him and marry him. The way you did with Jeremiah. And now I'm having second thoughts, I reckon."

Isabelle sat forward, reaching out to her friend across the table. She rested her hand on Brenda's. "It's okay for you to feel that way, Brenda. It is a big decision. And one you've had to think about a lot. You still have time to think about it and change your mind."

"But he's saying he's going to come here," Brenda said. "I don't want him to come here." She knew the emotion was strong in her voice. Fear that Isabelle wouldn't understand and would be offended by her reasoning because Clarice was her mother-in-law filled her.

For her part, Isabelle did look somewhat confused. "You don't want him to come here? But does that mean you plan to completely give up the cottage and move away forever? I thought you would come back and stay on vacation when you wanted to get away for a while. And you could bring your children after you have them to visit us."

Brenda liked the sound of that. She hurried to explain herself. "It's not that I don't want him to come here ever at all. Just not until after he meets me and knows that I'm not what the townsfolk here think I am."

She was surprised when Isabelle rolled her eyes and shook her head. "I've told you so many times, Brenda, no one here thinks bad of you. Well, Clarice and her friends might, but why do they matter? They don't know you the way we do. They don't care about you at all. You don't have anything to fear. When does he say he's going to come?"

"He wants me to write to him again. He doesn't say when he wants to visit, just that he wants to." Brenda sighed. She knew Isabelle's feelings on the matter but was still very hurt by the way Clarice and her friends treated her.

Isabelle sat back in her chair, her eyes on Brenda. "Tell me, my dear, when was the last time someone said something mean to you?" She tilted her head to the side, lifting her eyebrows. "I bet you can't even remember, can you?"

Brenda thought about it for a moment and realized she couldn't think of the last time. She knew who Clarice's friends were and didn't go into their shops or look at them when they passed, knowing she would be snubbed and her feelings would be hurt. She wasn't about to ruin her own day.

"I can't remember."

"Then stop remembering it ever happened at all," Isabelle urged her. "You'll be a lot happier that way."

## 7

Hendricks was a big man. He imagined he had a whole lot of blood in his body. Surely he had enough to keep him going until he at least got to that barn and rested his head, just for a little while. That's all he needed to recuperate. He'd been shot before and recovered just fine. He was young and healthy. This flesh wound wasn't going to kill him.

Still, the thought that he might continue to bleed until he passed out was frightening to him, and it took a lot to scare Hendricks Potter. He refused to let a minor injury take him down. He would go down fighting in the end, one way or another.

He took a deep breath, trying his best to ignore the searing pain that shot through him when he did so. It came from the movement he'd made, not from the breath he'd taken. He held it for a moment, closing his eyes, willing his wound to heal, or at the very least, to stop bleeding.

The barn was close enough for him to see it better now. The moon was bright, and his eyes had adjusted well. He slowed the horse so the movement wouldn't hurt so much. Getting down was going to be horrible. He didn't even want to think about it.

When he was close enough, Hendricks braced himself for the tremendous agony he expected to be in when he dismounted. He'd felt it before, and the adrenaline rush he'd enjoyed that got him through the initial moments of the injury was gone. Now all that was left was a tired feeling and an ache radiating through his body from the wound.

If Denver had been there, the whole situation would have been taken care of. The two of them could easily have apprehended all of them. He was an excellent shot and was completely fearless.

Hendricks prided himself on being a man of strength, both in heart and body. But being shot made him feel like a helpless little boy who really wanted the comfort of his mother's lap. He was much too old to feel that way, but he did. And he didn't tell anyone about it. Not even Denver. He could handle it himself.

He prepared himself, sucking in a deep breath and pivoting himself out of the saddle. He let out a loud grunt, especially when he hit the ground. He instantly went down to his knees, almost losing hold of the towel still pressed against his side. It burned like fire.

He crawled toward the opening of the barn. It had double doors, and one of them was hanging by one hinge, creating a large diamond-shaped entrance that allowed him to go straight through.

He was grateful to see there was still hay in the barn, though it was dusty and probably filled with vermin and insects. He told himself he should have brought in a blanket and wished he had the strength to go out and get one from the bedroll he carried with him everywhere.

Hendricks just wanted to rest. He could wish for all kinds of things. But all he could do was sit there and wait to regain some of his strength, which he was positive he would do. The wound wasn't as bad as it felt. The bullet had gone straight through the fleshy part of his side, missing every organ it could possibly have hit. He wasn't a doctor, but he was sure it hadn't gone in far enough to do any major damage. He wasn't sure why it was bleeding so much.

Or maybe it wasn't bleeding as much as he thought.

The barn was completely dark.

Hendricks turned his head and looked up at the wall beside the door, where normal people left a lantern on a hook so anyone entering would know where it was and be able to light it to see. He didn't hold out much hope. Even if there was a lantern, what were the chances it would have oil in it that would still light?

He had a matchbox in his vest pocket. All he needed was a torch or a lantern.

"Please God," he murmured, catching sight of a lantern on a hook. He would have to twist his body to get up and get to it. The thought of moving made him cringe. He braced himself and pushed to his feet, letting the pain out in a grunt of agony. He crept slowly the few feet and reached out for the lantern. To most people, it would have required reaching up. But at his height, he was able to get the lantern off the hook even though he was slumped over.

He fished the matches from his pocket, letting the towel hang loose inside his shirt. It only took a moment before he felt blood sliding over his skin. It irritated him. It made him want to get back on his horse and go to the nearest town doctor. Or at least a clinic where there were bandages and cleansing cloths.

He struck a match and held it to the lantern, turning the knob. "Come on," he murmured. "Come on."

It took three matches before the lantern lit, but when it did, Hendricks felt a tingle of satisfaction. He had pressed the towel against his side as soon as he had a hand free to do it.

He lifted it and looked around the barn. Now that he saw it up close, it looked more like a barn built less than a decade ago that had recently suffered damage, most likely from a lightning strike. Hendricks couldn't think of anything else that would make that kind of wreckage.

So this barn likely belonged to someone. If he didn't feel so much pain, if he wasn't so miserable, he would go out and find the house this barn belonged to. But he was slowly losing consciousness. He could tell.

The light from the lantern would draw attention, so he turned it down very dim. There was no logic in letting Kelsey and the others know where he was if he could help it. He didn't think they were still pursuing him, but he didn't want to take that chance. He got down slowly and sat with his back against the door. It was so painful, a feeling he remembered from the three times he'd been shot before.

He rested his head back against the door and closed his eyes, holding both hands over the towel, putting pressure on it. He said a quick prayer, asking for strength, before his mind began to wander. He thought about the last time he'd been shot. It was through his left leg, just underneath his knee. He'd been lucky in that instance, too. The limp he'd been left with was barely noticeable. No one ever said anything about it, and he didn't mention it. It was too slight to be merit mentioning at all.

That had been another lucky occasion for him. The two before that were both in the chest, just under his shoulder, and had occurred at the same time. His assailant, an outlaw he and Denver had been pursuing for a month, just wasn't a good enough shot. Denver had taken him down, and Hendricks hadn't thought another think about it.

Soon the light of the morning would come, and hopefully, someone would find Hendricks. An hour or two, he told himself. He could last that long. Surely he could last that long.

## 8

Brenda looked through the window at the bright blue early morning sky. It was going to be a nice day weather-wise. She felt rejuvenated. She'd made a decision not to write back to Leonard until she'd had time to think about it. If she didn't write to him, he wouldn't come.

She'd started a new row of beans in the vegetable garden and was expecting to be out there for several hours over the next couple of days as the beans were now ready to be picked. She had her wicker baskets ready. Then she'd take them into town and sell them by the bagful. It was a nice way to make a little extra money.

Her eyes sharpened on the distance beyond the garden. It was cleared out another twenty yards or so before the trees of the forest at the bottom of Crenshaw Mountain, which was behind her cottage.

Brenda narrowed her eyes, focusing on the woods in the distance. There was a building there. She'd noticed it before. It was a barn, she thought, that had been used by the previous owner but had been abandoned when a tall tree on its west side was struck by lightning. The top half of the tree caught on fire and toppled over, smashing into the roof of that barn. It hadn't been used in about six or seven years.

She wondered what, if anything, had been left in that barn. There was quite a bit of overgrowth around it but not enough to prevent her from checking it out. Plus, it was such a beautiful morning.

Brenda pulled a shawl around her shoulders and placed a wide-rimmed white hat on her head to shade her face. She already had her shoes on and went out the door casually, holding her cup of coffee, determined to enjoy the day. She was still happy about having received a letter from Leonard, even if she was on the fence about what to do about it. He'd complimented her, saying she sounded like an intelligent and sensible woman. She liked hearing that. She wanted to compliment him, too, but he'd given her no reason to. He'd said very little about himself.

One of the reasons why Brenda had chosen him was because he was so close to her cottage. She hadn't even thought about him coming to see her first. From talking to Isabelle, she'd assumed she would go to meet him first. He would send her a stagecoach ticket, and she'd hop in and ride off to her new life.

Why would he want to come and see her? She'd mentioned her friend had given her a cottage, but surely she hadn't made it sound so fascinating he had to see it. Maybe he wanted to do business with Jeremiah. She'd talked about him, too. She'd told Leonard about her father's arrangement, as well.

She hadn't focused on anything or given any negative opinions about what had happened to her. She hadn't talked bad about her father.

After analyzing what she remembered of her initial letter to him, Isabelle decided he was just highly interested in her. He was a little impatient. Maybe he was like that in most aspects of his life. She wouldn't know. He hadn't told her anything about himself. The letter had served its purpose and nothing more. She wondered if he thought he would be charged more with every word he wrote, like a telegraph.

She'd received a letter from Micah, too, but had kept that for opening when she was alone. She didn't read *all* her letters to Isabelle.

As she walked, staring out at the abandoned wreck of a barn, she saw something move. It caught her eye, and she froze in place. It made her gasp, and her heart skipped a beat.

It wasn't human. It was an animal. It was a horse. Even if it hadn't had a saddle strapped to its back, she would have been curious how the thing got into her backyard. It was someone's transportation. That was obvious.

She swallowed another sip of coffee, peering out at the animal. It belonged to someone. Likely someone who was around the barn area.

Her stomach twisted in knots. Was she in danger? Had her father sent someone to come and get her? Had Clarice and her friends hired someone to frighten her off her land and give up her cottage?

Wasn't that what she was planning to do anyway?

She hated the thought. She didn't want to leave her cottage. It was her home. She'd made it her own.

But she also wanted to be married and have children she could bring back to the cottage whenever she wanted.

Was that going to happen with Leonard?

She glared at the horse in the distance.

Or had her father sent someone to fetch her like some princess in a high castle?

She sighed, deciding to continue on. If there was someone there, she would have to trust she would be okay.

Brenda got closer to the horse, and it didn't move away. It was a friendly horse. She reached out when she got to it, mumbling softly, "I'm a friend, you see? A friend. I won't hurt you. You look big and strong. You belong to someone, don't you? Where's your master, huh?"

She patted the animal on the neck, moving slowly. It didn't move or attempt to get away. In fact, she felt like the bobbing of its head was to tell her something. The horse's large eye was focused directly on her. She stared back.

"What is it? Is your owner around here? Is he?" She assumed the rider was male. For all she knew, a woman could have been thrown from the horse and was lying around somewhere broken and hurt. "Hello?" she called out, looking around. She had a strong feeling there was someone in that barn since that's where the horse chose to stand. Had someone been seeking shelter? At least half that barn was intact and could provide warmth and a hiding place. "Hello?"

Brenda moved two steps away from the horse and stopped, her eyes drawn to something in the grass. She blinked rapidly, not wanting to believe what she was seeing.

There was a large splotch of blood a few feet away from her, and it was the first of several more that led to the barn. She followed the trail with her eyes to the edge of the barn and up the side of the door to the handle. The person had used a very bloody hand to turn the knob.

Brenda's heart nearly stopped. Her chest tightened. She swallowed hard and gathered her courage. Someone was hurt. She wasn't unaware of the danger she was putting herself in. But even if it was an outlaw or someone bad, that person was hurt, and she was not. She could fight for herself against a wounded person, couldn't she? Especially one who had lost so much blood.

She pulled in a deep breath and forced herself to walk straight to the door. It was open enough for her to simply push on it so it would swing wide.

**9**

———

Brenda crept into the building, which had dark shadows created by the light streaming from the hole in the roof. She immediately spotted the man in the corner. His head had rolled to the side. One hand was against his side, covered in blood. The other was on the ground next to him, palm up. His legs were stretched out in front of him. Other than the bloody wound on his side, he didn't appear to be injured.

Brenda stood for a moment, hesitant about approaching him.

"Hello?" She said the word in a quiet, gentle way. He didn't stir. She took a few cautious steps closer, peering closely at him. "Hello? Mister? Are you all right?"

He still didn't move. She took a few more steps and was now only a few feet from him. She could see his chest rising and falling, so she knew he was breathing. But his eyes were closed, and he hadn't moved an inch.

"Mister?" She reached out and touched his shoulder. He still didn't wake up. When she pushed him a little harder, he began to slide to the side. "Oh!" She grabbed him before he could hit the ground and lowered him gently, so he was lying on the ground, his wounded side exposed.

Brenda took her time and very gently checked the injury, lifting his hand and setting it in front of him. She pulled the towel away, barely touching it with the tips of her fingers. She didn't want this strange man's blood all over her hand.

It was still seeping. She let out a frightened breath, jerked the shawl from around her shoulders, and replaced the bloody towel with it, tossing the towel to the side. Her shawl began to absorb the blood. She wondered why it hadn't stopped bleeding. Had this just happened? She wondered how long the man had been there.

She studied his face while holding the shawl against the bullet wounds, one in front, one in back. He had hair as black as midnight, even darker than her own. Hair had grown from his chin and upper lip, but it was obvious he regularly shaved and just hadn't had the time to do so in a while. There were stress lines around his eyes. She wondered if he was in pain.

He was quite a large man. She wasn't sure she'd be able to move him. But she couldn't leave him here in the barn.

She thought hard for a moment. There had to be a way to get this big man back to her cottage so she could help him. Leaving him here was not an option. Waking him up didn't seem like it was going to work. She looked down at him again, feeling the pulse of his body under the hand she was using to press the shawl against the wound. She felt heat. Somewhere in the back of her mind, she remembered hearing that wounds that were hot weren't a good thing.

Panic struck her. She didn't want this man to die right here in this old barn. He looked young, other-wise healthy. There was no way for her to know for sure, but she didn't get a sense of danger from him.

"Think, Brenda," she sighed, whispering to herself. "Think."

A sudden thought came to her mind. She jumped up and hurried out the door. Nearer her house, there was a newer barn and storage shed she used. Brenda moved quickly to fetch the wheel-barrow and bring it back.

Once she had the wheelbarrow inside the barn, she contemplated how she would get him in it. She thought of using ropes to pull him in, but that didn't seem logical. She eventually titled the wheelbarrow on its side right next to him and spent the next ten minutes rolling the man into it. It had tall sides, thank goodness, so once he was inside it and she was able to get it up on its three wheels, he was less likely to fall out.

She was amused that the man's horse followed them. She felt encouraged by the calm demeanor of the horse, which seemed to realize she was helping his master.

Brenda struggled mightily with the wheelbarrow and pushing the heavy weight of the unconscious man back to her house. She didn't care that the sides of the wheelbarrow scraped the doorjamb as she went inside. She had to stop halfway through to move his arm so it wouldn't bump against the wall.

She pushed the wheelbarrow into the living room and stopped right next to the couch. Now she had to get him onto it.

Before she attempted that maneuver, she grabbed some clean linens from the pantry. She spread a blanket over the couch and set a pillow on one side for the man's head.

Brenda stood back and studied the task she had before her. How to get the large man from the wheelbarrow to the couch without either of them getting hurt in the process. She tapped her lips with one finger, thinking.

Finally, she saw what needed to be done. Really the only solution she had.

She pushed the wheelbarrow so that it was directly adjacent to the couch. She drew in a deep breath and held it, shoving the wheelbarrow over so that the man fell out onto the couch. He didn't look comfortable at all when he landed.

Brenda shoved the wheelbarrow away from her and moved to adjust him, making him more comfortable. Before she drew a blanket up over him, she checked the shawl trapped under the man's shirt. The bleeding seemed to have lessened now. She was surprised by how pale the man was.

Once she felt he was comfortable enough, Brenda ran out to get her own horse ready. She rode into town to the clinic to fetch the doctor without hesitation.

The clinic wasn't far from her cottage. It wasn't until she got there that she realized she might have a little trouble. The reason was the nurse. Marge Crabtree. Marge was a good friend of Clarice's. She was one of the women who looked down their noses at Brenda, sure that she was an entitled brat looking for money.

The doctor wasn't like that, though, she told herself, and he was the one she was going to get.

But Dr. Anderson wasn't there. She saw with dismay that the clinic buggy was gone, which likely meant he was in it.

She went to the clinic anyway. The nurse had dedicated her life to helping people, hadn't she? Surely she would be compassionate enough to help the stranger in Brenda's house.

Brenda went to the clinic, happy to see she was the only one in the lobby. Marge was behind the desk as she came in and gave her a blank look.

"May I help you?" she asked, sounding like she didn't want to help Brenda at all.

"A man has been wounded and is in my cottage. I need Dr. Anderson to come and help as soon as he can. Do you know when he will be back?"

"The doctor won't be back for some time. You will have to take care of your man yourself."

Brenda shook her head. "He's not my man, he's just wounded, and I have him in my house. I found him in my barn out back. I need the doctor to come as soon as he can. Will you tell him?"

The woman gave her a disdainful look. "Do you assume I will not do my job? You will have to tend to that man on your own until he gets there."

Brenda stared at the woman, feeling like a mouse about to be stepped on. "All right, thank you."

Why was she disarmed by this woman? She'd taken care of wounds before. Now she would again. She'd stop by the pharmacy and get what she needed. She wished she hadn't even stopped at the clinic, knowing the doctor wasn't there.

**10**

———

The pharmacy was close enough to the clinic so that Brenda could walk to it. She pushed open the door and immediately looked to see who was working. The owner, Elizabeth, was another friend of Clarice's. But her husband, Elmer, wasn't. He treated Brenda with the same respect he did anyone else in Low Branch.

"Good morning, Brenda."

She jerked in reaction to Elmer's booming voice from the other side of the store. She spun around, a smile on her face, relief flooding through her.

"Elmer. Good to see you. I need some help real quick."

"Tell me what you need." The man strolled over,

his girth taking up all the space between the aisles of goods.

"I found a... there's a..." Brenda didn't want to tell him she'd brought a man into her cottage, a strange man who had apparently been shot. "I need something to clean wounds."

"For humans or animals?" He eyed her up and down, probably checking for wounds. She chuckled.

"For humans but not for me. I'm fine. But I might get hurt. If I hurt myself, what will I do? What would I do?" She hoped he'd give her some extra advice. She hadn't studied how to tend to gunshot wounds. She'd just paid attention when others in her life had been hurt and were taken care of by someone else in the field, not in a clinic setting.

"What kind of injury are you talking about?" Elmer asked curiously. She could tell he was wondering what she was going on about. She wanted to tell him. But it was bad enough she'd spilled it to Marge, who was sure to tell Clarice, who would spread around even more vicious gossip about her.

She decided to go out on a limb. "I'll tell you, Elmer, but you have to promise not to tell anyone else. Not the sheriff or anyone."

Elmer looked completely taken aback, his white,

puffy eyebrows shooting up, wrinkling his forehead. "I promise," he said in a grim voice. "Whatever you have going on, Miss Brenda, I'll be glad to help."

Brenda was surprised by the kind offer. She was sure most people in the town thought very little of her. The rumors Clarice had spread were awful.

"I... I need to know how to clean a gunshot wound," she stated plainly.

She could tell Elmer was trying to hide his shock. His eyes were moving around the room rapidly.

"You don't say," he murmured.

"Yes. Do you know what I need?"

Elmer seemed to come to an acceptance of what he was being told. He finally met her eyes again and nodded curtly. "I do have what you need. Right over here."

Brenda followed him to a small shelf near the register that displayed bandages and healing ointments. She eyed everything available, unsure how much she would need.

"I'll help you." Elmer reached to the side and grabbed a wicker basket from a pile there waiting to be sold. He began to put several of each item on display into the basket. "You'll need this and this and this."

He snatched up a thin book that was as thin as a pamphlet and threw it in the basket. "Suggestions and instructions for anyone to know how to treat a gunshot wound. You have to do different things depending on where the shot is at, you know. Some parts bleed a lot more profusely than others."

Brenda nodded. "Yes, I think I understand that."

She pictured the bloody towel, the shawl she would need to throw away, the strange man's own shirt, and her ruined couch.

She'd left the man unconscious in her cottage. She was anxious to get back there. She allowed Elmer to put whatever she would need in the basket and paid for it all, during which time she read through the section on treating gunshot wounds. She was amazed that the small book had instructions on what to do for different parts of the body. The torso—as it was put in the book—was a vulnerable spot because of all the organs that could be hit.

Since Brenda wasn't a doctor, she could only do her best to make sure it was treated the best way she knew how. When Dr. Anderson actually got there, she wanted him to be proud of the work she'd done.

More than that, she wanted to save the man's life. He'd looked so pale as if there was very little blood left in her body.

"Best of luck with your venture," Elmer told her as she left with her supplies. She gave him a warm smile.

"Thanks for helping me with this, Elmer. And the person I'm helping would probably also want to thank you, too."

Elmer just nodded. "Good luck, dear."

Brenda left the pharmacy, heading back to her horse. Soon she was back at her cottage, leaving her horse out front to get inside to see if the man had woken up.

He hadn't. He was still lying in the same position she'd left him in an hour before.

She took the basket of bandages and ointments to him, took a deep breath, and settled in to do what she could for him. The side that was hurt was up, so she was able to gently pull his shirt away and remove the bloody shawl.

The wound was still oozing, was hot to the touch, and was surrounded by pink skin on the front side. The back looked almost unharmed, other than the hole where the bullet had exited.

It was the entrance hole that was giving him the most trouble. That was where it wouldn't stop bleeding and looked like an infection was brewing. At least, that was Brenda's estimation. She really wished the doctor had been available. Feeling another quick tingle of irritation because Marge wouldn't have helped even if she could, Brenda carefully began to treat the wound.

She thought about what she would accomplish that day while she worked on him. He didn't flinch or move while she did so, even though she had to touch his injury to wipe it clean and put the bandages on.

He was still unconscious when she was done. She sat back and surveyed her work, proud of herself. He was still breathing, and as long as the doctor came to check on the wound and make sure it wasn't really infected or treated it if it was, the man should be just fine.

## 11

Hendricks woke up surrounded by blankets. He didn't feel dirty and sticky like he had when he'd last been conscious. His first thought was that he'd been found and was now in jail for trespassing. But there was a slim chance he would have blankets all around him if he was in the jailhouse.

He slowly opened his eyes, gazing more and more at what was around him. It was a large enough room, with a few chairs, two couches, a fireplace, and some side tables. A round rug on the floor greatly enhanced the comfortable atmosphere he was surrounded by.

When Hendricks was awake enough, he tried to sit up, expecting pain to slice through him from his side. He put his hand down to keep the wound from opening or bleeding more and rested his hand against a perfectly placed bandage. He was in pain but not a tremendous amount. He didn't even need any alcohol to kill it.

He rubbed his chin with one hand, peering around the room he was in. It was someone's home, and he was betting it was a woman. A woman who lived alone. He saw nothing masculine about the house, and there were no toys around or signs that a child was ever there. It was too clean.

He grinned. He didn't know anything about children himself, but he'd been in the homes of families with children, and there was almost always a sign a child lived in the house.

He pushed the thick blanket off him. It was a bright sunny day. Heat was coming through the window beside the couch he was lying on. He was parched.

There didn't seem to be anyone in the house with him, so Hendricks slid out of bed and, crouched over slightly, went to the door of the room and looked out into the small foyer. To his right, another doorway appeared to lead to a short hallway. There were two doors in the hallway facing each other. One was open, and the other was not. He left the room behind and went to the open door in the hallway.

It was the kitchen.

Hendricks grinned. How perfect.

He went to the cupboards to get a cup for some water. The sink to his left had a pump fit right to the side of it. He was impressed with the convenience and wondered how much it had cost to get something like that put right into the house. The woman must have plenty of money.

He reached up with his right hand to grab the handle of the cupboard door. Pain slipped through him like a knife blade. He grunted and dropped his right arm, using his left instead.

Grumbling that he shouldn't have hurt himself like that, Hendricks took a cup from the cabinet and went to the sink.

Again, he naturally grabbed the pump with his right hand. The motion sent him into more pain, and he nearly doubled over. He rested both arms on the side of the sink and hung his head, reeling from the agony. It took him a minute to recover. When he thought he could move again, he pushed up, so he was standing straight. He'd been gripping the cup in his hand so hard his knuckles were white.

He relaxed his fingers and switched the cup to his right hand to pump the water in with his left.

Gritting his teeth together, he watched the water splash into the cup, longing for it more than he'd ever thought possible.

He drank three cups of water before he felt refreshed. When he was finally satisfied, he set the cup on the counter next to the sink and turned away from it. As he did so, his eyes caught sight of something out of the kitchen window.

In the garden out back, a woman was standing, swaying from side to side. He frowned, pulling his eyebrows together. What was she doing? He moved slowly to the window and stood there, staring out at her. She was a beautiful sight to see. In fact, Hendricks was positive he'd never seen a woman with so much beauty about her before.

Her long black hair trailed down almost to her behind. She was slender and looked fit and strong. She probably took care of the cottage herself. He wanted to know what else was around here. Was it a working farm? Was she there when the barn was hit by the tree struck by lightning? Was she friendly, or had she just done her duty by taking care of him?

His thoughts raced through his mind, random and sometimes silly. He wanted to go right out and talk to her, but the thought of moving that much and going that far intimidated him.

It was an unfamiliar and unwanted feeling, but Hendricks had pushed himself before when he'd been injured and knew that it simply wasn't worth it. The doctor he had seen had advised him to stop putting so much pressure on himself and his body. He needed to recover since he was just a human being like everyone else, despite the dangerous job he'd chosen.

He told himself these things as he stood at that window, looking out at the woman.

Hendricks wondered what her name was. He was very curious about her, even though he would find out all about her when she came back inside. This was her home, after all.

He turned from the window and looked around the kitchen. Simple and clean. Just like the rest of the house that he'd seen so far. She had very few decorations but what she did have was beautiful, elegant, and classy. He was impressed.

Turning back to the window, he noticed that she'd turned around and was tossing seeds on the ground around her, following a pattern line. She had the sack of seeds strapped around her shoulder and was holding it still with one hand while she dug into it with the other.

His heart fluttered in his chest. She was astoundingly beautiful. Long, black eyelashes framed her eyes. Her lips were red, and her high cheekbones were flushed with exertion.

Hendricks's heart nearly stopped. He couldn't wait for her to come in and talk to him. He felt like banging on the window to get her attention, but that would probably scare her to death. He cleared his throat and then chuckled at himself for thinking she would hear him from all the way out in the garden.

To his astonishment, the woman looked up directly into his eyes.

He froze. So, apparently, did she. Her arm was even still extended to throw the seeds to the ground.

He wasn't sure about the look on her face when she caught sight of him. At one moment, she looked thrilled to bits, which made him feel amazing inside. Then there appeared a moment of fear, probably when she realized she'd let a wounded strange man into her house, and now he was awake.

But there was something else he saw on her face that surprised him. It looked like happiness. She looked happy that he was standing there in her house.

**12**

B renda was only using seeding the garden as a way to distract herself from the fact that she had a man in her cottage. An unconscious man who would be awake soon, God willing. Or was it? If he should die, Brenda would never know what kind of man he was or why he had been shot. Who could have done such a thing to him?

When she turned around to spread the seeds down the row behind her, she abruptly saw him standing in the window. She blinked at him for a moment, unable to keep from freezing, at least for a moment.

Then she lifted her hand and waved at him, her expression unchanging.

He smiled at her. That was all it took. He lifted one hand and placed it on the glass between them. The small gesture yanked at Brenda's heart, pulling her heart strings almost out of her chest. She stopped seeding immediately and gestured that she would come inside. Then she stopped and gestured if he wanted to meet her, making a circle with one finger and mimicking the two of them meeting in front of the house.

He nodded.

She liked him already. He understood her sign language.

Curious to know who this man was and what had happened to him, Brenda hurried to the front of her house, pushing open the door the moment he got there to the other side, coincidentally.

He kept his smile, backing up so she could come inside.

"Howdy," he said quietly.

She came into the house and stopped right in the foyer, looking at him warily.

"Hello," she responded. "Are you... are you feeling all right?" She couldn't even think of the right words to say. She could have kicked herself for asking such an inane question. Of course he wasn't all right.

"As good as can be expected, I reckon," he answered naturally. "I think I better go back to your couch, though, before I pass out. I got up for water."

"Yes, yes," Brenda agreed, nodding. She pushed him gently to turn him around and directed him to the living room. "Let me put a fresh blanket underneath you so you won't be around any of that blood. I couldn't change it until you woke up. You're a little bigger than me, and I wasn't strong enough."

"Strong enough to get me here from the barn, though."

She could hear how impressed he was with that. It made her feel good inside. She smiled at him.

"I did," she said simply. "I might be a genius."

Her quip must have caught him off guard because he gave her a look of surprise and delight at the same time. "You just might be," he agreed. "Thank you for helping me. Not a lot of people would."

"I wasn't going to let you die out in my barn, that's for sure."

"I appreciate that," he said with a chuckle. They were in the living room at that point, and he grunted loudly as he lowered himself to the furniture. She pulled the blanket from underneath him before he settled down, making him laugh softly. "I apologize. You did say you were going to do that, didn't you?"

She smiled at him, liking him already. "My name is Brenda. Brenda, if you're a friend."

"I'm not a foe," he replied, maintaining his smile. She suspected it wasn't just from nervousness, but he did look a bit anxious to her. "The name is Hendricks. Hendricks Potter."

He held out his hand, holding himself up on the armrest. She shook it, appreciating that he didn't grip her hand too firmly. "Brenda Watson. And yes, please do call me Brenda."

She balled up the blanket and took it to the pantry, where she had a basket she used to put dirty clothes in. She dropped the blanket in the basket and grabbed another. There was only one left. She hadn't been expecting to use any of them and really didn't have that many to begin with.

When she returned to the living room, the first thing she noticed was the look on his face. He was extremely uncomfortable. It would be better for him if he was laying down, she surmised.

"Would you like to sit on this couch instead?" she asked. "Or lay on it?"

She intentionally spread the blanket on the second couch, which was directly opposite the first against the wall facing the window. He raised his eyebrows.

"I reckon it doesn't matter which one." She saw him glance down at the one he was sitting on. He recoiled visibly when he saw the blood on the edge of the cushion. It had streaked down to the actual couch frame. He instantly looked ashamed, which pulled on her heart.

"It's okay," she said quickly, coming over to help him to the other couch. She held her hands out to him as she came over, partially to comfort him when he saw how much blood he'd spilled and also to help him stand if he needed her. "I was going to throw that couch out anyway and get a new one." She hoped he didn't catch on to her lie. The look he gave her said he was a little suspicious. He would be right. She'd had no intention of getting rid of the couch.

But it had been there, according to Jeremiah, for years already, having belonged to the previous owner. The cottage was in perfect shape when she moved in, and some of the furniture had come with it. She felt no particular attachment to the piece of furniture since she hadn't picked it out.

She felt the previous owner would understand

what had happened if they were there to witness these circumstances.

"Well, if you say so," he murmured, taking one of her hands. He grunted as he stood up but was silent as they crossed to the other couch.

She got him comfortable and laying down. He was noticeably eased when he was lying down, to the point that she heard a relieved sigh come from his lips.

He laid back on the pillow and closed his eyes. She stared at him, wondering if he was going to sleep. He opened one eye and peered through it at her. "I'm not sleepy," he said. "I've been unconscious for some time, so I don't expect to be sleepy. You haven't given me any kind of medicine, have you?"

She shook her head. "I have nothing here," she replied. "Not even liquor. I went to town to get supplies. I should have picked some up then."

Hendricks blinked at her. "What, liquor?"

She nodded.

He shook his head briefly. "Nah," he said. "I don't need any. Don't need to be drunk. I've got to stay on my toes. You don't think I shot myself, do ya?"

She could tell it was a rhetorical question. She didn't see how he could still be in an amiable mood after getting shot, smiling and joking.

"No, I don't think that," she answered, "but I always thought that's what men needed when they got shot."

He grinned. "As opposed to women?"

She scrunched her nose at him. "No, women, too."

"No women?"

She rolled her eyes and had to laugh. "All right, Hendricks Potter," she said firmly through her laughter. "No liquor for you. Is there anything else I can get you?"

"Right now, I'm just grateful you helped me. I have to thank you. You've stitched me up good."

Brenda shivered, picturing his skin as she'd drawn the needle and thread through it. How he'd stayed unconscious while she did that was beyond her. It had to have been incredibly painful.

"I've done my best," she replied. "So you can't go gallivanting around until you get that checked out."

"I won't do any gallivanting. I promise," Hendricks responded.

**13**

———————

Hendricks couldn't believe how at ease this woman seemed around him. He was a foot taller than her and twice as wide. She was small and petite compared to him. But he could also see how strong and able-bodied she was. It was an utter delight that she didn't seem intimidated or frightened of him.

Once they'd introduced themselves, she'd gone to the kitchen and returned a few minutes later with a cup of coffee for him and two biscuits with ham and slices of cheese in between the top and the bottom. He eyed the food hungrily but took the coffee first, taking a few swigs of the drink, which was hot but not too hot.

He wolfed down the food, trying not to eat too quickly, but he was famished.

"Thank you so much," he said when he was done, handing the plate back to her. She'd stood in front of him the whole time he was eating the biscuits, so he knew it hadn't taken very long to eat them. He gave her a sheepish look, but she shook her head, understanding what he was thinking. She had beauty and brains. He was highly impressed once again.

"No, no," she said gently, giving him a warm smile. "I knew you'd eat those that way. I have more food and more substance for you because you'll need to build up your strength. Those two were just to start because if I gave it all to you, you might have eaten it all the way you just ate those two biscuits in twelve seconds flat."

He heard no malice in her voice.

"I'll get you some more food and bring it in here, and you can tell me what happened to you."

Hendricks could tell there would be no way of getting out of that. She wanted to know the truth, and he was going to tell it to her, whether he liked it or not. He waited until she was out of the room to grin and shake his head. She was so small, and yet he felt a force around her that made him want to obey whatever she wanted him to do.

She was a little lady who had already grabbed his heart.

The next moment, Hendricks's mood abruptly changed. He thought of Denver and Kelsey Bradshaw. He'd been shot by someone in that group with Kelsey. The outlaw wasn't alone anymore. And he could have followed Hendricks to the woman's cottage, too. Just because he hadn't shown up yet didn't mean he wouldn't track Hendricks down. That meant Brenda would be in danger, too. Because of him.

With an aching heart, Hendricks realized he would have to leave. He couldn't do that to the woman who had saved his life. Putting hers in danger wasn't a fair reward for what she'd done for him. He didn't want to tell her right away because he knew he needed more recovery time before he went to town to get a room and visit the doctor. That only made him nervous, which made his heart beat faster, and the pain in his side flared up because of the worry running through his body.

She came in a short time later with a bowl of beef stew that was as big as her head. Several slices of bread from a loaf had been set beside the bowl on the plate it was on, which she set down on the coffee table in front of the couch.

Hendricks painfully pushed himself to a seated position, holding his hands out for the bowl, eager to fill his empty stomach. He lifted his eyes when she didn't immediately give him the bowl to see that she wasn't looking at him. When she did, she hurried to give him the bowl.

"I'm sorry," she said gently, in a voice that made his heart melt.

He shook his head. "It's okay. I'm just hungry, is all."

She giggled, setting the bowl in his hands. She turned to grab one of the bread slices to give him as well. "I only cut these two slices, but if you want more, just let me know."

He nodded. His mouth was full as he spooned the stew in, chewing the bits of meat and potato, reveling in the delicious taste of it. He swallowed and gave her a grateful smile.

"This is wonderful. You're a good cook. I could get nice and healthy eating your food."

She blushed, which made her even prettier in his eyes. She smiled back.

While he was eating, Hendricks thought about how quickly his depressed, anxious mood had vanished the moment she walked back in. It might have been because she brought food with her. But he suspected it was something else.

Maybe getting shot was the best thing that ever happened to him. It had brought him here. Maybe it was God's will that he found the woman of his dreams by first getting hurt and making her take care of him.

His thoughts made his mood lighten even more, and he chuckled, glancing up as Brenda went to one of the two smaller chairs in the room near the fireplace and pulled it over closer to him so she could sit facing him.

"I'm really sorry about your couch, though," Hendricks said, gesturing with his head at the bloodstained furniture across from him. She glanced at it, quickly moving her eyes back to him. He could tell she didn't want to look at it. He didn't believe for a moment that she was about to get rid of it anyway, but it was cute that she'd tried to say that to make him feel better.

"It's really okay," she said, using his word to emphasize her point. "The couch is old. It isn't something I picked out myself and wasn't given to me by anyone special. It's just a piece of furniture. I'll get something new."

Hendricks couldn't help pulling in a satisfied breath. He knew he was stalling. He didn't want to tell her what had happened to make him come to her home injured and bleeding, a complete stranger, relying on her not to be afraid of him but to offer him help instead. Again, he got the feeling it was God who had sent him there. It just seemed too coincidental for it not to be.

"I do feel bad," he replied, "but if you are sure, I won't mention it again."

She nodded at him. "I'm sure. You don't even think about it. I'm curious to know why you were shot, though. What happened to you? Are you... you're not an outlaw, surely."

He laughed, shaking his head, noting the relief on her face. "I'm not an outlaw. I'm a bounty hunter. And that's how I got shot."

**14**

———————

Brenda was more than comforted to hear he was on the right side of the law. She sat in the chair watching him eat, thinking about what the people in town would think of her letting a stranger into her house. He wouldn't be able to stay, and that was enough to make her feel bad. Why should she have to make him leave just because of what people in town would say?

It wasn't a good way to try to recover her reputation, though. And what about Leonard? What if he just showed up out of the blue one day and announced he was there to take her to marry him? Her father would be on board for that, Brenda was sure. She was just grateful her father didn't even know what she'd done.

"Tell me what happened," she said gently. "How did you end up getting shot?"

As he spoke, she thought about how smooth his voice was, how calm he seemed talking about being attacked by the men with the outlaw he'd been seeking.

"I didn't know he was with anyone. I'll be honest with you, Brenda, he never has been seen with anyone before. Not ever. So it was unexpected, but I wasn't too bothered by it. The only problem I had was that my partner wasn't with me."

She was surprised to hear he had a partner. Was it a woman? The inflection in his tone didn't seem to make it sound like it was a woman. If it was, she would have expected to hear more of a gentle tone. He said "partner" like the sheriff said "deputy."

"And where is he?" she asked.

"We split up." She was pleased she had guessed correctly. He continued, "Kelsey, the guy we're after, Kelsey Bradshaw, he disappeared on us and forced us to choose between two paths he might have taken. We really thought he'd go to a bigger city and try to meld in with them, hide in the crowds, you might say. But we do know that he doesn't like the big city and prefers the smaller towns. So I got the short straw, which meant I checked the smaller places while Denver went to Richmond."

Brenda nodded. "I know of Richmond. Someone who doesn't like crowds would not want to go there."

Hendricks snorted, a knowing look on his face. "It was foolish of us to think he might even want to hide in the crowds. He clearly doesn't care about hiding. He'd rather be out in the middle of town square shooting at anyone trying to apprehend him than cowering in the corners while lawmen pass by."

Brenda was impressed with the way he spoke. He seemed well-educated, which was not something she encountered very often, especially not when talking to lawmen. They always seemed so focused on the physical aspects of life, they didn't have time for academia.

Not this lawman. She wondered if he'd gone to college.

There was so much she wanted to know about this man.

"Where was it you saw him last? Close by? Do you think he knows you came here?" Brenda wondered if she should be scared. Looking at Hendricks, sitting in front of him, she wasn't scared. She didn't even care if this Kelsey Bradshaw was outside. And she didn't care that Hendricks had been the one who left their last encounter wounded. She wasn't afraid. Hendricks wasn't just big. He was smart. She had no doubt he would figure out what to do.

Besides, she'd learned how to shoot a gun when she was eleven. She wasn't a sharpshooter, but she was darn good at aiming and hit her target square in the center 75% of the time. She was proud of that accuracy, especially because she never had an opportunity to shoot unless she went out to do so on purpose.

Hendricks was probably the kind of man who would enjoy going out to shoot at targets with her. She smiled thinking about it.

"This was the best stew I've ever had in my entire life," Hendricks said, coming to the end of his bowl. He tilted it up and swallowed the last bits that slid out into his mouth. Running the back of his hand over his mouth, he handed the bowl over to her. She took it but set it on the coffee table.

"Do you want more?" she asked.

"I've had enough for now," he replied, grinning. "Thank you so much for that. I really can't tell you how much better I feel. You've tended to my wound, listened to me talk, and been an excellent companion. I hate to have to leave."

Brenda's heart plummeted in her chest. She didn't want him to leave. Even though she knew, for both their sakes, he had to.

"You're not going anywhere yet," she said firmly, standing up after picking up the bowl again. "You have to rest. You won't make it out there, especially if Kelsey Bradshaw is waiting for you."

Hendricks's eyebrows shot up. He gave her a complimentary look, and she couldn't help wondering what it was for. "I figured if he knew I was here, he'd come and get me."

Brenda thought quick and replied, "Not if he doesn't know I'm the only one who lives here. You said he usually travels alone. Maybe those men he was with weren't his traveling companions. Maybe he didn't join their gang and was just stopping in to drink with them or something like that. So if he followed you, he likely did so alone. I might have a husband in here. Or I might live with my father and three brothers."

She loved the way he let out a delighted chuckle. "In a house this small? Not a chance."

She laughed, too, shaking her head. "All right, so my father and one brother. He isn't from around here, so he doesn't even know I live here probably. Is he reckless? Wouldn't he watch until he thought it was safe to come out?"

Hendricks blinked at her. "But if we follow your logic, that means I can never leave."

Brenda struggled not to burst out laughing. If only it could actually happen that way. But no, he would have to leave the house eventually.

"Since you're right about that," she continued, "I insist you stay for another few hours so you can rest up. I don't want you stepping outside that door until you feel well enough to go right into town and talk to Dr. Anderson. The clinic is just inside town on the fourth right building after you get there. You'll see it. There's a big red cross above the door."

Hendricks nodded. "All right. I'll stay for another couple of hours. Then I'll go into town. Just like you said."

Brenda stifled a sigh. She had another few hours with the man of her dreams. Then he would leave, and she would probably never see him again. He was a bounty hunter. He was always on the road. He might even die soon at the hands of a criminal.

She didn't want that to happen. She had to see him again. If it was up to her, she would see him a lot in the coming future.

It wasn't up to her, though. Much to her chagrin,

his job required him to leave town in pursuit of dangerous men and, on rare occasions, women. It would be his decision. She would just have to make it hard for him to leave town, she thought. Make it hard for him in the nicest way possible.

15

---

"What about you?" Hendricks asked, curious to know more about this woman that had saved him. "What is a nice young woman like you doing living all the way out here in the middle of nowhere by yourself?"

Brenda laughed. "This is not the middle of nowhere. It's only a half-hour walk to town. I have neighbors. You just can't see them for the trees."

"Oh, I like it," he said quickly. "I hope I didn't cause offense."

She maintained her grin, shaking her head. "No, not at all. I'm teasing you. It's a nice little cottage, isn't it? My friend Jeremiah bought it for me." She leaned forward, a mischievous look in her eyes. He was intrigued, leaning toward her, as well. "I had to come here from Frontier because my father was trying to make me marry someone I didn't want to marry."

"Uh oh," Hendricks blurted out. "That's not a good thing then. Didn't like this fellow, huh?"

Brenda's facial expression told him how she felt before her words did. Her eyes went soft, and she tilted her head slightly, looking up at the ceiling. "Oh, it wasn't that." Her voice was soft. He was confused. She almost looked like she had feelings for the man she'd run away from. "He was a friend of mine. We went to school together. Our fathers were... are best friends, and so they just thought we would be the perfect match. But, alas, Micah is in love with another, and I so want him to be happy."

Hendricks felt bad for her. He'd never been in a situation where he was in love with someone who was in love with someone else. He'd never been in love to begin with.

"I'm so sorry to hear that. You couldn't work anything out? You had to run away?"

Brenda pulled in a deep breath, nodding. "Yes. I had to leave. My father was insistent. They think that because Micah and I get along so well that we must be in love. Or that we will someday fall in love with each other. But I'm telling you the God's honest truth, Hendricks, Micah and I are not and will never fall in love. It hurts me to think my father wants me to do that to Lydia when she is such a sweet girl." The woman grinned. Hendricks was amazed at her. She was so honest and truthful. He could tell there wasn't an ounce of regret or vindictiveness because the arranged marriage hadn't worked out. It was obvious Brenda and Micah were just what she said—very good friends.

"I assume you tried to talk to your father about it all?"

"Yes, but they wouldn't listen." The corners of Brenda's lips turned down in a cute way that tugged at Hendricks's heartstrings.

A thought came to his mind for the first time since he'd woken up. He jerked a bit, and pain split through him. He settled back, realizing he really wouldn't be able to leave for a while. The pain would prevent him from defending himself if Kelsey was out there waiting for him.

"My horse. You didn't happen—"

"I got him," she said quickly, dousing his fear. "He's in the barn with mine."

Hendricks relaxed into the back of the couch. "Thank you," he murmured.

"You're in pain, aren't you?" she asked, concern in her tone.

He nodded. For anyone else, he might have denied it. Something about this woman made him feel free to be open with her. He could be vulnerable in front of her. He didn't have to act like his size.

She made him feel five feet tall and skinny as a rail.

It was an exciting and strange feeling.

"Don't worry about me being in pain," he said, dismissing it with a wave of his hand. "I wouldn't be alive if you didn't find me. I'll take the pain over death any day. It's not bad enough to make me want the end to come."

She laughed. He wanted to, but the abrupt movement had made his wound flare up, and it was aching now. At least he was aware of it. He'd forgotten about it while talking to her, even if only for a few minutes.

"Tell me about your little town," Hendricks said, cocking his head toward the front door. He didn't know if that was the right direction, but it didn't matter. She wouldn't care, and he knew it. "Do you have a lot of nice people like you living here?"

She looked thoughtful and didn't immediately gush about the townsfolk, which both amused and surprised Hendricks. He cocked his head to the side and waited for her answer.

"Well," she said slowly, "I can't really tell you as much as you'd like to know probably. I'm not from here. I only came in March. That's when my father was trying to marry me to Micah. I got this cottage in May... well, that's when Jeremiah bought it for me."

Hendricks raised his eyebrows in surprise. "Oh, so you really are very new to this cottage." He swept his eyes around the room, wondering how much of it reflected her personality and how much had been left behind by the previous residents.

"Yes, I come from Frontier, as I said, and that's a couple of hours away, I guess. By stagecoach. Jeremiah is my friend, and he's wealthy and married to a lovely lady who runs the garden shop in town. She often helps me with my garden, even though I tell her she doesn't have to take time out for me. She says she wants me to feel welcomed by her since I'm so new and have no other friends to come and visit."

Hendricks was impressed with the friend's wife. "That's very nice of her."

"I strive to be like her in many ways," Brenda responded, settling into the chair across from him. He could tell she was enjoying his company and the conversation as much as he was. He relaxed against the couch and let himself appreciate the soft voice of the beautiful woman across from him. "She's a nice person, very smart, generous, and kind. That's the kind of person I am and want to be more of every day."

"That's so nice," Hendricks remarked. He was beginning to wonder if this woman was even real. Surely she had no flaws whatsoever. "I'd like to meet her."

Brenda giggled, her smile wide and pretty. "You can. Just go to the garden shop in town and tell her you met me."

Hendricks gazed at her. "I'd rather not go alone. You know her so well. Maybe you can come with me?"

Brenda looked startled for a moment. He wondered what she was thinking that had made her expression change so drastically.

"I... I don't know if that's a good idea."

Hendricks pulled his eyebrows together. "Whyever not?" he asked.

She just shook her head. It was the first strange moment between them, Hendricks thought, and he didn't particularly like it. He wanted to go back to how he'd been feeling about her a few minutes before.

"It's just better that way," she said. "You'll understand after you talk to her."

He blinked and stared at her, unsure what that meant but now desperate to find out. He would visit the garden shop before anywhere else in Low Branch.

16

Brenda made sure Hendricks stayed throughout the day. She made them lunch and had a bowl of stew for him in a container to take on the road. She didn't want him to leave until dusk so that he would have to go straight to town and get a room. Otherwise, he wouldn't be able to see.

What she really wanted was for him to stay the night. And there were several reasons for that. It wasn't just that she knew he would be better off not moving for a couple of days so he could heal faster. She also felt like he was safer in her house, and she was safer *with* him in the house.

By her way of thinking, if Hendricks left and Kelsey was watching outside, he could always decide to come in and kill her for helping Hendricks. Then he might pursue Hendricks, catch him off guard and wounded the way he was, and finish the job.

The very thought made her aggressively push for Hendricks to stay longer each time he readied himself to leave.

But eventually, he had to go. She set him up with a lantern in case he didn't get to town in time, but she felt strongly he would make it. The sun wasn't due to set for another hour or so by her estimation. He would be in town long before that.

It was a strange goodbye. He kept hesitating and stopping on his way out the door, across the porch, and down the six steps. She had already prepared his horse. She even cleaned the horse, taking off his saddle and brushing him down while Hendricks slept inside during the day they'd spent together.

She stood with him next to his horse. He glanced at the animal with wary eyes.

"I'm dreading getting up in this saddle," he mumbled.

She felt for him and gave him a soft look. "I know. I'm sorry. I wish I could help."

"You have. So much," he exclaimed quickly as if he had to let her know as vehemently as he could.

She just smiled, holding his gaze. Was she

supposed to give him a hug? That seemed illogical considering he was injured and a little forward on her part, as well. She couldn't just let him get in the saddle without doing something, so she awkwardly held out her hand to him, grinning.

"Well, you just take care of yourself now, Mr. Bounty Hunter," she said playfully. "It was nice getting to know you, and I hope we get another chance to talk when you haven't been shot."

He laughed appreciatively. "Yes. I agree. It was a nice day, despite the pain and, you know, everything else that's happened to me in the last day or so."

"You're looking a lot better," Brenda remarked, "but you have to go to Dr. Anderson and get checked out. So make sure you do that first thing in the morning, okay?"

She wouldn't be satisfied until she knew he was going to get the care he needed. Plus, she was a little curious to know what the doc thought of her stitching job and the overall care she'd given him. The little pamphlet-style book she'd gotten from Elmer really turned out to be a great help.

Hendricks plopped his hat on his head and tilted it to her. "Yes, ma'am," he replied. He turned to the horse and pulled in a deep breath. Brenda couldn't help pulling in a breath of her own and holding it while he got up in the saddle with a mighty grunt. Her hand went up behind him as if she had any control at all and would be able to catch him if he fell.

Once he was in the saddle, he looked down at her. He must have seen her concern because his eyes softened. "You've been wonderful to me, Brenda. Really. Thank you so much. I'm sure we'll see each other again."

*Until you leave for another job*, she thought to herself, *or to go find Kelsey.*

Thinking about the outlaw made Brenda look around, scanning the trees for movement or anything out of place.

"I better get going," Hendricks said. She returned her eyes to his face, wanting to pull him back out of the saddle and carry the man, though twice her size, right back into her house.

"Be careful," she replied instead. "And make sure you go to the clinic tomorrow. I'm going to ask Dr. Anderson if he's seen you. So be mindful of that."

Hendricks's slow grin and gradually raised eyebrows amused Brenda. "You're going to check up behind me?"

She nodded, keeping her eyes directly on his. She wanted to know what his reaction would be to that. He blinked, looked away for a moment, and then back at her. "All right, Brenda. I'll go. I give you my word."

"That is good enough for me," she said, holding out her hand one more time. He shook it and gave his horse a gentle nudge to get him moving.

Brenda watched the horse and rider leaving her behind to feel alone and cold in a place she'd never felt like that before. In fact, Brenda had always been comfortable with her own solitude, even before she came to the cottage.

Now she felt like she might as well go in and go to bed. Nothing exciting was going to happen for the rest of the day anyway.

Brenda stayed there for a few more moments, watching until he was out of sight. It didn't take long since he'd gone through the forest down one of the trails. She'd made sure he knew where Low Branch was from her house and which path to take. She was banking on the fact that Kelsey didn't know anything about the area. She had no way of being sure, but she was praying pretty feverishly.

As long as she didn't hear a gunshot, she told herself. She also thought maybe she should go after him at a distance, just to make sure he was all right.

When the irony of what she was thinking struck

her, Brenda had to laugh. She was a tiny little woman who could shoot a gun like any other average person. He was a bounty hunter by trade, a huge man by most standards, with intelligence, strength, and courage. He didn't need her to protect him.

Regardless, she felt the urge to do so, the need to make sure he was healthy, safe, and happy. In Low Branch, he would be at least two of those things, and that made her feel better.

It seemed so ironic that he had shown up in her barn that way. She'd been longing for marriage and a husband but not to Micah. This was what her father didn't understand, she thought. Now this man came along and was almost dropped into her lap. Was it divine intervention?

Brenda went back into her house without looking around anymore. She would only terrify herself if she kept thinking about Kelsey coming to get her. She would go to town tomorrow, first thing, just to make sure he'd gone to the doctor and gotten his wound checked out.

## 17

Hendricks winced as Dr. Anderson slowly peeled the bandage away from his gunshot. The doctor sucked in through his teeth, which alarmed Hendricks.

"What?" he asked. "What's wrong?"

"This is a nasty wound, Mr. Potter. How did you get it?"

Hendricks tried not to be annoyed. Brenda had spoken highly of this doctor.

"I got shot," he replied bluntly, following it up with, "I'm a bounty hunter, doc. This happens. It's happened twice before. Here, here." He pointed to the places he'd been shot.

"You don't need to explain yourself further, Mr. Potter. I understand now. Please let me look this over. You say the Watson girl did this? Brenda Watson? That's Jeremiah's friend, isn't it? I mean, she is."

Hendricks let out an amused breath. "Yeah. Brenda. You know her?"

"I do." The man's voice had a strange inflection to it. Hendricks looked at him pointedly.

"What does that mean?" he asked, referring more to the way the doctor said the two words than the words themselves. "You sound like there's something off about her."

He didn't want to think she was an outlaw in disguise. There were a few women who went against the laws of common society, and those that did usually didn't regret it, nor did they pretend to be grateful for any help they might be receiving. They were greedy, spiteful, vindictive women who didn't mind cutting off the hand that fed them and spitting in the eye of their loved ones.

Hendricks had met two such women. He wanted to avoid being taken advantage of by a woman like that. And he had no doubt in his mind Brenda was not like that. That kind of woman wouldn't have done for him what she did for him. She wouldn't have saved his life. She would have raided his pockets to take whatever she could from him.

"Miss Brenda has gotten a bad reputation around this town, and she was done wrong by that."

Hendricks frowned. Brenda had a bad reputation? How was that even possible?

"Please explain. I'd really like to know how the people of this town don't love her to death."

Dr. Anderson stepped away from him to write something on a chart. "She did a fine job on your bandage, Mr. Potter. You can tell her that the next time you see her."

Hendricks's thoughts were interrupted by the sincere desire to see her again. And soon.

"As for our Miss Brenda," Doc continued, "it was that Clarice Connelly that did that to the poor girl. She's... that is Brenda, she's got history with the Connelly family, y'see. Mr. Jeremiah and Mrs. Isabelle Connelly. The missus runs that garden shop down the street. You ever need seeds or advice on growing, she's the one to go to."

Hendricks nodded. "I'll keep that in mind," he said, while at the same time wishing the man would hurry up and tell him.

"Clarice didn't like the look of her, I reckon. She took right up in her face, just'a talking, and complaining. Then she told her son the same things right to *his* face."

"And what happened?" Hendricks asked, fully invested in the story at that point.

"Oh, Jeremiah went and kicked the ol' woman out."

With that, Dr. Anderson burst out laughing. Jeremiah got the distinct impression he wasn't impressed with the "ol' woman."

"What did she say about Brenda?" Hendricks asked, sitting up straight while the doctor redressed his wound.

"I'm really surprised by how well she did this," Dr. Anderson murmured, his head down by Hendricks's side as he removed the old bandage completely and used a long cotton-tipped swab to clean off the sides of Hendricks's skin. It felt like the doc was scraping Hendricks's skin with something sharp. It made Hendricks tense up, closing his eyes and clenching his jaw. "Real sorry about the pain, Hendricks. Let me give you a morphine tablet. That will make you feel better quick. Then I'll finish cleaning this up and redress it for ya. These stitches will want to come out, and they'll probably wiggle their way out of your body before we get to them. Either way, you come back in here in four days so I can check it. If you aren't in town, go to the doctor wherever you are."

Hendricks wanted to be in Low Branch. He felt as if he'd just been given the go-ahead to stay.

"Oh, and Clarice... she said Brenda was looking for a man with money and had turned down fine gentlemen because they weren't rich. Those kinds of things. Strings men along. Only one problem with that."

Hendricks gave the man a curious look as he buttoned his shirt. He was a bit cold.

"What's that?" he asked.

"Nobody else sees that. She can't string men along if she's never on the arm of a man."

That made complete sense to Hendricks. He nodded. "So the woman was just being jealous of a younger woman coming to town."

"I reckon. Not like Clarice had anyone clamping onto her."

Hendricks had never heard of it put quite like that. He gave the doctor an amused look. "Clamping?" he said with a chuckle.

The doctor shrugged, turning away from him to jot something down on his paper. He wrote whatever it was and looked up at Hendricks. "If you knew Clarice, you'd know why I used that word. It's more that she'd be clamping onto someone else. Like some kind of... I don't know, clamping monster.

She's pushy. Bossy. She's got her friends, and those are the ones who make Miss Brenda feel bad about herself."

"That's a real shame," Hendricks said. "She seems like a real nice gal to me."

"She is," the doctor replied, coming back with a fresh bandage to put over the stitches and ointment. He finished his work and stood up straight, looking directly at Hendricks. "Been a real shame she hasn't been clamped by some man in Low Branch."

Hendricks burst out laughing, which sent a sharp stab of pain through his side. "Doc," he cried out, holding his side with both hands. "That wasn't nice."

The doctor grinned. "Sorry about that, young fella. I couldn't help myself. You probably shouldn't laugh too much. It might hurt."

Hendricks gave the doctor a mischievous look of warning. "All right now, give me my boots, and let me get out of here before you make me bust through this thread."

He pushed off the bed and stood up to his full length, almost dwarfing the doctor, who looked up at him. "Make sure you let that girl know I think she did a good job. She seems very nice to me, and I'm glad she was able to help you out."

"Thanks, doc. What do I owe you?"

"You can settle up with Marge out there in reception. And don't say anything to her about Brenda. That woman is one of Clarice's good friends and will fill your head with nonsense. Waste of your time."

"All right, thanks again, doc."

## 18

Brenda passed the clinic on her way to the garden shop, pleased to see Hendricks's horse out front. He had gone to the doctor just like she suggested. Of course, it would have been quite silly for him not to have gone. He didn't need her to tell him to do it.

She hummed a soft tune as she approached the garden shop. She could see Isabelle inside through the square, four-pane window to the left of the door. She was smiling and talking to someone, but the customer was hidden by the wall and not visible through the window.

Brenda pushed open the door and stopped as soon as she stepped in, stunned to see the customer was Hendricks. She should have known by the way Isabelle was looking up. Hendricks towered over her friend the same way he towered over Brenda.

"Well, howdy," he greeted her exuberantly, his smile wide and friendly. Brenda knew what Isabelle was thinking just by the way her friend looked at her. She was impressed with Hendricks, too.

"Howdy," Brenda responded. "Isabelle. How are you this morning, honey?" She went to her friend, who was behind the counter, and leaned over the top to give Isabelle a hug.

"Oh, it's been a good morning. I was just talking to Hendricks about you."

Brenda wasn't surprised by her friend's blunt admission. They obviously hadn't been saying anything bad about her, or Isabelle likely wouldn't have mentioned it at all. If Marge at the clinic had said those words to her, she would have gotten a different impression.

"And just what was said about me, might I ask?"

"The doctor said you did a great job stitching me back together," Hendricks said.

"Is that so?" Brenda couldn't help the pride that came through her voice and the big smile on her face.

"That's so," Hendricks confirmed, smiling back.

"Whatever you did when you redressed it kept the infection away. Doc said it looked like it would have gotten infected if you hadn't cared for it properly. Mostly because I laid in that dirty barn for hours till you found me."

"Thank God I did," Brenda replied. She glanced around the shop. "I thought I'd pop in and see if you have anything new and interesting."

"Not since yesterday," Isabelle teased. "But you know you don't need to buy something when you come here. I'm just glad for the company." She turned her eyes to Hendricks. "Doc told this fella he has to stay in town for four days, isn't that right, Hendricks?"

Brenda loved how quickly Hendricks was making friends. The thought of Doc demanding Hendricks stay in town seemed pretty strange to her, but if that was the case, she was grateful to the man.

"Oh? Why? Not that I don't want you here, that's not it at all. I've just never heard Dr. Anderson tell anyone they shouldn't leave town."

Hendricks didn't seem to mind the suggestion. From the look on his face, Brenda surmised he'd taken it as good advice. Her thoughts raced through her mind. She wanted him to stay in town so she could get to know him. But she'd already started the ball rolling elsewhere. Would these two collide?

Brenda silently chided herself for assuming things were the way she wanted them to be in her mind. There was no guarantee Leonard would ever show up in Low Branch. There was also no guarantee that Hendricks was or could fall in love with her.

She was getting ahead of herself. It was time to slow down and take stock of what was happening to her at that moment in time.

She smiled at Hendricks and Isabelle. Being with a friend and making a new one was her current circumstance.

"Why don't you show Hendricks around town, Brenda?" Isabelle asked in an encouraging way. "He doesn't know anyone. And since you told him about Clarice, I reckon you'll know just who to introduce him to."

Brenda blinked at Hendricks. She hadn't expected him to talk to Isabelle about that particular issue. "Well, I wish I was a fly on the wall ten minutes before I came in. It seems you two have had an extensive conversation about me."

Isabelle grinned, shaking her head. "Not at all. As a matter of fact, he'd just come in a few minutes before you and said, "I believe your name is Isabelle. You aren't one of the ones Clarice said bad things about Brenda to, are you? You're her friend."

Brenda glanced at Hendricks again, this time with a soft expression. "Did you really say all that? To introduce yourself?"

"I'm afraid I did, Miss," Hendricks replied. "I hope you don't mind. You just seemed so comfortable when you spoke about Isabelle. I knew she would be able to direct me where I needed to go and was hoping we'd have a good conversation in the meantime. Which I believe we have, haven't we?" He looked at Isabelle, whose pleasant expression and quick nod confirmed what he'd said. "See? Your friend is now my friend."

"I'd be happy to show you around, Hendricks," Brenda said. "The first thing we can do is go to the boarding house to make sure you have a room and don't have to stay in a strange woman's cabin every night. That might not look good for you or the person who's helping you."

"I agree with that," Hendricks responded firmly with a curt nod.

"And you must promise to ignore all the bad and nasty looks you might see coming my way. Mostly from old ladies. Can you do that?"

To her surprise, Hendricks looked contemplative. He tapped his chin with one finger and his hat against his leg, almost in rhythm. "Well, I think I can refrain from leaping on old ladies for giving you a bad look. If you want me to, of course."

Both ladies laughed. "Thank you kindly, young man."

Brenda laughed harder at Isabelle's joke. Hendricks was older than either of them.

She held out her hand to him. "Shall we go look around?"

Hendricks looked taken aback by the offer of her hand. It was her intention to only take it until they were at the door of the garden shop. She hadn't thought about the impact his touch might have on her. She had to turn away with one last smile at Isabelle before hurrying to the door, almost in an effort to let him go quicker.

Her heart was racing uncomfortably. She was as nervous as could be, shaking like a leaf. She didn't want to see the anxiousness in her eyes, so she looked at the door she was heading toward.

Brenda found great relief in letting him go but, at the same time, immediately missed his touch. She dreaded what the ladies and men who already thought bad of her would say when they found out she'd let him stay in her cottage overnight?

Brenda felt like she was doomed if she did and doomed if she didn't. When it came to Hendricks, though, she was willing to take the risk. He was well worth it.

**19**

———————

The sun bounced off Brenda's black hair making it look violet, drawing Hendricks's attention to it. She was small, shorter than him, and stylishly slender. The light green dress she'd chosen was perfect for the spring day, in his opinion, and looked good on her.

"I'll get a hotel room instead of the boarding house," he said, flipping his eyes between the two buildings, which were down the street to the left, the hotel on the left side of the street, the boarding house on the right. They weren't opposite each other, but they were fairly close together. Hendricks assumed that was because everything that could be bought, sold, bartered, and banked was right there in the Low Branch town square. He figured by the look of it, the business area of Low Branch must have taken up at least a mile of the main road with roads expanding from it to carry business outward.

Low Branch would be a booming town one day, Hendricks thought to himself.

"I guess it doesn't really matter. Whatever you want to do, Hendricks." She smiled at him. He'd been surprised when she took his hand in the garden shop, less surprised when she let it go as soon as they got outside. The sensation of her touching him lingered in his mind and made his hand tingle when he thought about it. He wished she had never let go.

"What are you going to show me first?" he asked, pulling in a deep breath and scanning the street with interest. People were coming and going, many of them laughing and chatting while others looked serious and solemn. An apple cart near them was brimming with fresh red apples, making Hendricks's mouth water. He glanced at Brenda before tapping her on the arm. "I'm goin' over there," he said, pointing, and crouching a bit, so he was closer to her. "I'm gonna get me one of them apples."

"They do look good, don't they?"

Hendricks and Brenda walked around Low Branch for the next twenty minutes. They started on the right side of the road and went down two blocks before crossing and coming back to where their horses were. Hendricks munched on his apple till it was down to the very last bit on the core before throwing it away. He kept his eyes on the people around them. It didn't take him long to notice the ones who had low opinions of Brenda. The look of disdain on their faces irritated him. He was willing to bet they hadn't gotten to know Brenda at all before they made their judgment call. Based simply on the word of a bitter old woman.

It was infuriating.

Fortunately, it was only a handful of people. Everyone else either looked with uncaring eyes or smiled at them. He was impressed with the town. It seemed like a friendly place to stay and have a family and raise children.

Hendricks was surprised by his own train of thought. Never before had he thought about settling down. Ninety-nine percent of his brain power was used on work matters. He thought about Denver more than he thought about any woman in his life.

But that was before. Before he got shot and was rescued—literally his life was saved—by the beautiful woman walking next to him. He'd been blessed, and he didn't know why.

"I see ice cream," he said at one point, noticing a small shop at the corner of the street. The girl behind the counter was leaning on it, gazing flirtatiously at the young man on the other side. "Looks like someone else had the same idea."

"Oh?" Brenda was using a teasing tone that made Hendricks struggle not to laugh before she'd even said anything. "Were you thinking of going over there and saying something to that young lady? She's a little young for you, isn't she?"

He let out the laugh he'd been suppressing, shaking his head at the same time. "She is definitely too young, and I mean... er, I'm saying..." He was flustered, which made him blush, which made him more flustered. He let out a frustrated sound but laughed afterward. "Never mind. Let's get some ice cream."

He could tell Brenda was having a good time. She almost looked like she was glowing. It was a good look on her.

They purchased two cones and sat on a bench underneath a big Oak. Hendricks looked up to make sure there weren't any birds over his head before he sat down.

As soon as he was seated, he spotted a young man running in their direction. He watched for a moment to see if he was really coming toward them before jostling Brenda's arm with his elbow. "You know that kid?" he asked, pointing. "I think he's coming over here."

Brenda looked where he was pointing. Her eyes lit up but only for a second. "That's Eddie. He works with the Postmaster. Looks like he has a letter for me."

Hendricks turned his eyes back to the boy, wishing he'd sent Denver a letter from Low Branch. He was very curious about where his partner was. He hadn't heard from him in way too long.

Eddie waved the letter over his head as he came closer. "Brenda," he called out. "I have a letter for you."

Hendricks was curious about Brenda's behavior as Eddie came closer. He could see how unhappy she was. She had become stiff, and he noticed she was kneading one hand with the other. She was suddenly a bundle of nerves. What kind of terrible letter was she expecting?

Eddie handed it over to her. Hendricks's eyes dropped instinctively to the letter. He looked away quickly but caught the name on the return address before he did. It was a letter from Micah. Seeing that, he lifted his eyes to look at Brenda for her response.

The look of relief and delight in her delicate features made Hendricks even more curious. Who had she been expecting a letter from? Her father?

Hendricks chided himself for his overzealous curiosity. None of this was any of his business. If he was courting the beautiful woman next to him, that would be a different story. But for now, her business was not something he was privy to. He respectfully turned his eyes away, smiling at Eddie. "You want a tip?" he asked, fishing in his pocket for a nickel, which he produced and handed over to the teenager. "Here you go. Thanks for that."

"Thank *you*, Mister," Eddie said with a grin. "Ain't you that Hendricks fella? The bounty hunter?"

Hendricks was caught off guard. He blinked at the boy, nodding. "Yeah, that's me."

He jabbed one thumb over his shoulder. "We got a telegraph for you. A message from someone named Denver. It's back at the office. I can go fetch it for ya."

Hendricks was a little surprised by how excited that news made him. He nodded vigorously. "Please do that. I'd appreciate it."

"You got it, Mister."

Hendricks watched Eddie spin around and bolt down the road. The boy was a fast runner. In no time, he would return with the note from Denver. So his partner knew he was already in Low Branch.

He took a moment to wonder how that could be.

# 20

Eddie was back with the printed note a minute or so later, handing it proudly to Hendricks as if he'd taken it himself. For all Hendricks knew, the boy *had* been the one to do it. Who was to say he didn't know the code?

Hendricks read what was on the paper. It was short and sweet. Denver was in Richmond. He'd been searching for Kelsey. He received Hendricks's confirmation that Kelsey had gone that route and was heading for Low Branch. It was dated before Hendricks got to the small town, which told him Denver would probably be there soon. He'd sent the note in advance of his arrival to be given to Hendricks whenever he arrived in town.

It was good to know his partner was alive and on

his way. He must have stayed in Richmond an extra day or two. By his calculations, Hendricks figured Denver should already have arrived in Low Branch.

"So what does your friend have to say?" he asked Brenda, who was fanning herself with her letter, her eyes gazing out in front of her, a pleasant smile on her face. He felt a tingle run through him when she turned her green eyes to him. They were so bright, flanked by long dark eyelashes that fluttered at him and made butterflies burst through his stomach.

"He's having a devil of a time getting our fathers to come to reason. He hasn't given up on Lydia, thank goodness. He's talking about coming here to Low Branch to live just to get away from them." She giggled. He didn't understand why until she continued. "The funny thing about that is that he would come here with Lydia after they are married in secret, and our fathers would probably think he was moving here to be closer to me. They don't understand a thing about a friendship between a man and a woman. I don't think they think such a thing exists. What about you? Do you think a man and a woman can be friends without anything else coming into it?"

Hendricks had to think about it for a moment. It wasn't something he'd ever thought about before. He pondered it before answering, "I haven't had any real relationships with women. Not courting or seeing each other socially, nothing that would have led to marriage. So I have to believe it is possible. Otherwise, I would have had fifteen or sixteen wives by now."

He was delighted when she burst out in laughter. "Oh no. That would be terrible. And I will write to Micah and tell him your view on it so he can use that with our fathers. It's very good."

He grinned. "Thanks. I don't have to ask your opinion on the matter. You're living proof, aren't you?"

She leaned her head to the side, a starry look in her eyes. "I suppose I am. How wonderfully bizarre." She came out of her thoughts just seconds later, turning her gaze to him. "And what about you? You got a message from your partner. He's alive!" She clapped her hands lightly, holding her ice cream cone between her fingers.

"Yes, thank God he's alive. I was beginning to wonder."

"Is he coming here to meet you?"

"Yeah." Hendricks looked up and around him. "I would have expected him here by now. I'm gonna go talk to the sheriff. Haven't seen him yet. Maybe he's heard from Denver, too. Gotta check-in anyway. Let them know Kelsey is around Low Branch."

She nodded up at him as he pushed to his feet. Pain slid through his side, and he did his best to ignore it.

"The sheriff's name is Carl Bancroft. He's a good man. You'll like him. He is good to anyone who's on the right side of the law."

"That's good to hear. You going home?"

"I think so. I'm not sure yet. I'm going to talk to Isabelle first. Then I might go home. I do have some work to do in the garden."

"I'll see you later then?"

"You can come over whenever you like. Thank you for spending the morning with me."

Hendricks's chest tightened as he took a step away from her. He didn't really want to leave her, but he did have work to do. He would have to arrange a few random "meetings" with her. Surprise her by just showing up wherever she was.

He chuckled, which made her eyes dart to his face with a suspicious look.

"What are you thinking?" she asked in a teasing voice, narrowing her eyes at him.

He shrugged. "Just hoping we get to meet up

again and talk soon. The ice cream was good. The company was better."

She tilted her head to the side, giving him a sweet look. "What a nice thing to say. You go take care of your business. We'll see each other again soon, I'm sure."

He had to chuckle again. He was willing to be directed by her, told what to do, instructed. He didn't mind it a bit. Anyone else and they would have had a problem.

This little lady could tell him what to do anytime she wanted to.

He waved at her as he headed for the jailhouse. She stayed where she was, just watching him leave. It made him feel a little strange, but he kind of liked it.

When he turned to go into the jailhouse, he glanced back at the big Oak to see she was no longer there. He moved his gaze back and forth until he spotted her. It appeared she was heading back to Isabelle's shop but had stopped to talk to an older gentleman on the way.

Relieved that she seemed okay after their morning together, Hendricks pushed open the door of the jailhouse and stepped inside.

He was immediately met with a rush of hot air

that was gone as fast as it came. There were two desks in the main room and a door that probably led to cells in the back. A set of wooden stairs went up to the second floor, which took up only half the building, with rooms built above the cells. The ceiling in the main room was the same height as the second-floor ceiling, so it was quite high.

Hendricks looked up, noticing a skylight had been installed, and the rush of hot air probably came from there when he opened and closed the door, changing the air pressure in the room.

"Howdy." A man with a deputy badge on his dark brown vest walked over to him, one hand out, the other placed firmly on the butt of his gun. He was looking up at Hendricks, searching his face. Hendricks wondered if he was trying to recognize him. He probably thought he'd seen Hendricks before, and it was likely. He'd often been in the papers but had only had one picture ever published of himself. Otherwise, the artist's depictions were what were used.

"Howdy." Hendricks shook the man's hand. "Lookin' for the sheriff."

"He's in his office. You can follow me. You're that Hendricks fellow, aren't ya? Bounty hunter?"

Hendricks nodded. "Yeah, that's right. Hendricks

Potter. Been following Kelsey Bradshaw. You fellas know anything about him?"

"I'm Deputy Allan King," the man replied. "Jackson Creek right there." He pointed to another deputy. "Follow me. I'll let the sheriff know you're here. As for this Kelsey Bradshaw, we've heard of him. He's comin' to Low Branch?"

"I don't know if he's coming here. I know he's in the vicinity right now. Or I'm assuming he is." By the time these words were out of his mouth, he and the deputy had gone into the sheriff's office.

**21**

———

A week had passed since Brenda had saved Hendricks's life, and she was still thinking about it and about the man himself nearly all hours of the day. She didn't get a lot done anymore, finding herself staring out in space thinking about him, wondering how he was doing, what he was doing.

She wouldn't let herself think about the possibility that Leonard might just show up out of the blue. She hadn't received any letters since the last one and hadn't written him back in the hopes that he would find another woman to court. It was only one letter she'd written to him. Surely there were other ladies interested in him. He wasn't a pauper, after all, and seemed nice enough from his original ad and the letter she'd received.

Brenda hadn't forgotten, though, the uncomfortable feeling she'd gotten when she was reading it. She didn't know the man and had never heard his voice. But something about the tone of the letter didn't sit right with her.

Or maybe she'd just sensed she was going to find what she wanted and needed if she was just a little bit patient.

Brenda chuckled deep in her throat. She was standing at the front window in Isabelle's shop, watching her friends and neighbors pass by. She watched as Eddie ran down the street with two other boys tossing a watermelon between them.

"They're gonna drop that," she mumbled. They tossed it skillfully and made it further than she'd thought they would before the big melon plummeted to the ground and smashed. She let out a groan for them and thought what a waste it was. The boys didn't see it that way, apparently, because they took the largest pieces and ran off down the road, eating through the red, juicy inside.

"What's wrong?" Isabelle asked from behind her. She turned around and strolled over to sit on a high stool next to her friend. Isabelle was trimming the leaves of a small plant, a tiny tree of some kind that Brenda didn't recognize.

"Oh, Eddie and his friends just smashed a watermelon in the middle of the street."

"Those boys," Isabelle replied softly, her focus on the tree in front of her. "Look at that. How does that look?"

She stepped back and surveyed her work. Brenda did the same, admiring the technique and skill Isabelle had. "You really do now what you're doing, Isabelle," she remarked, taking a few steps to the left.

"Thank you, Brenda. That's sweet of you to say and completely predictable. What else would you say after all?" Isabelle smiled and winked at her, moving forward again.

"You're right. But that doesn't make it untrue. I couldn't do that. I don't think I'd have the patience. I barely have the patience to keep my own garden going. You're going to have to help me, Isabelle. That's all there is to it."

Isabelle lifted her eyebrows. "You know I will be happy to help you whenever you need it, Brenda. It'll get me out of this shop, too. Jeremiah says I need to get out and enjoy my life more. But I don't know. I'm enjoying it a lot right here with my plants." She scanned the room with loving eyes. It was nice to see her friend so passionate about something. Isabelle sighed softly. "I suppose being outside with plants would be better for me anyway. That's what Jeremiah says I need. More sun."

Brenda watched Isabelle resume her clipping. "My friend isn't overbearing, is he?"

Isabelle glanced at her with only her eyes. "Overbearing? Jeremiah? Never. If you mean he pushes me to do things or demands I do things a certain way. He's not like that."

Brenda was relieved. "That's good," she said. "I've never known him to be that kind of person, not even when we were younger. I'd hope he wouldn't grow into a man that treats his wife shamefully. Jeremiah has always struck me as the kind of man who treasures the ones he loves. He's going to be an excellent father, you know."

Isabelle blushed. "I know," she whispered.

Brenda studied her friend's face. "You're thinking about it, too, aren't you?"

It had been over a year since Jeremiah and Isabelle wed. He had never mentioned to Brenda if they wanted to start a family, but why would he? She barely spoke to him over the past few years and only reconnected with him when she needed help getting away from her father. Jeremiah didn't mind the absence. He knew he could have reached out to her anytime. They were both aware that life had taken them in different directions for a time. Now they were together again, their relationship rekindled, new friends found.

"Yes. I think I might be now."

The revelation came in such a quiet voice that Brenda wasn't sure she heard right. She leaned closer to Isabelle. "Did I hear you right?" she asked, excitement growing in her chest.

Isabelle's blush deepened when she turned her eyes to Brenda. "I do think so, Brenda, I really do. But I haven't confirmed it yet."

Brenda hopped off the tall stool and practically threw herself at Isabelle, wrapping her arms around the woman's shoulders and squeezing her tight.

"Oh, oh. I'm so happy for you. I can't believe it. Though I *should* believe it, and I actually *do* believe it." She laughed at herself, excited to the point of fumbling her words. She held Isabelle in front of her at arm's length, looking the woman in the eye.

Isabelle laughed, graciously receiving Brenda's congratulatory hug. When she pulled away, though, she had a skeptical look on her face. "Please don't tell anyone yet, Brenda. I don't know if it's true. I haven't been able to verify it with Dr. Anderson. It's more like a feeling. I just... I'm just hoping and praying."

"Surely a woman would know," Brenda gushed. Her enthusiasm overflowed and made her a little giddy. "I guess I wouldn't know myself either and would have to ask. If it was your fourth or fifth, you wouldn't even be questioning it, would you? Mind you, I'm not saying you have to have that many. But, Lord knows, if you want that many, it's impressive. You don't even know what one is like yet." She laughed, realizing she was rambling. She gave her friend one more hug before hopping onto the stool again, where she sat restlessly, shifting back and forth and crossing and uncrossing her legs.

"I think you might be more thrilled about this than I am," Isabelle said with a laugh as she returned to grooming her tree.

Brenda grinned. "*I'm* not going to have it. *You* are. I'm about as thrilled as I can be for you, but I'm not ready for anything like that. Oh, Jeremiah is going to be over the moon with happiness."

"I hope so."

"You hope so?" Brenda didn't understand that thinking. "Why would he not be thrilled to death?

This is his child. He loves you so much. I'm sure he's looking forward to it happening."

Isabelle was quick with a response, "Oh, yes, I know. He will be so very happy if I really am going to have a baby. But he's such a worrying man. He's always worried about me as it is. Right now. Without being pregnant."

Brenda giggled, nodding. "That does sound like Jeremiah. I can't wait till you tell him the good news."

## 22

Hendricks stood in front of the mirror, staring into his own dark brown eyes. He slicked his hair back with one hand and lifted one side of his lips in a cocky grin. "Well, howdy, pretty lady," he practiced, winking at himself.

He was a bundle of nerves. He wasn't the kind of man who didn't express himself, and holding in what he was feeling for Brenda was driving him out of his mind. He straightened his tie, smoothing it down his shirt to follow the line of buttons.

He stepped back and surveyed the finished job. He looked nice. Church was starting in forty-five minutes. He would get there early and hope she was coming, too. She usually went with Jeremiah and Isabelle, and they always seemed to be there early.

He wanted to talk to her.

All morning, Hendricks had been trying to plan what he should say. It seemed like everything that came out was just wrong. It was disappointing and disheartening.

But Hendricks wasn't going to let it get him down. He might not be amazing with his words, but he was sure she'd understand his intent. If he gathered all his courage, he was sure he could find the right words. God willing.

When Hendricks left his house that morning, he was completely unprepared. At least, he felt that way. Two hours of on and off mirror practicing hadn't seemed to open the portals to his language skills.

He prayed silently as he walked toward the church at the end of the street. There were several people out front, which meant they couldn't yet get inside. That was a bit strange since the pastor was in the little house next door, and there was no reason for him to be late. He might have slept over, Hendricks presumed, but even then, it was less than an hour till it was supposed to start. Surely someone had woken him by now.

All these thoughts passed through Hendricks's mind as he walked toward the building. He forgot about his questions when he saw Brenda walking with her friend and Isabelle. Jeremiah was between the two women, talking animatedly. He was gesturing with his hands while the two ladies flanked him, their small hands wrapped around his elbows. They both had smiles on their faces, which made them look radiant to Hendricks. Both were beautiful women, and despite knowing it as a fact, neither was haughty or put on airs.

The three seemed to look at him in sync, and their following smiles were warm and friendly. He saw a teasing expression come to Jeremiah's eyes. He couldn't help wondering if Brenda had said anything to her companions about him. What could she have said? From the look in her friend's eyes, it wasn't anything negative. That made Hendricks feel good inside, and his confidence was boosted.

"Howdy," he called out. "How are my good friends on this bright Sunday morn?"

"It's a good day to be alive," Jeremiah responded, holding out one hand.

The ladies both curtsied just slightly at him. Brenda's fluttering eyelashes weren't lost on him. The look made butterflies explode in his stomach. Hendricks shook Jeremiah's hand, nodding at the ladies, pulling the hat from his head and setting it back down as a salute to them both.

"I agree wholeheartedly," he replied. "I was wondering if I might sit with y'all at church today. If ya don't mind, of course."

"You know we don't mind," Jeremiah responded, his eyes flicking to Brenda, that secret smile still plastered on his face.

Hendricks hoped Jeremiah didn't consider his thoughts a secret because he was making it obvious to the world. He approved of the budding relationship between himself and Brenda.

Hendricks liked that very much. From what Brenda said, her father might require some extra effort. But he was willing to do it. He'd do whatever it takes. He was looking forward to meeting her family.

Brenda looked a little bit nervous. He wondered if she was thinking about the same thing. Did she have butterflies in her stomach, as well?

"What are you doing after church today?" he asked, looking at Brenda directly. She was wearing a dark blue dress that brought out the color of her eyes, accentuating how dark her hair really was. "I thought the four of us could go on a picnic."

"That sounds lovely," Brenda gushed, turning to

her friend. "Oh, let's go on a picnic this afternoon. I bet it won't even be very hot."

Jeremiah grinned, giving Brenda what Hendricks considered an odd look. "Brenda, why are you asking me permission? You can go on a picnic with whoever you want whenever you want. You don't need me to go with you." With that, he turned his gaze to Hendricks. "And to answer your question, sure, I'm sure Belle and I would love to go on a picnic. Can't answer for this one, though." He jerked a thumb at Brenda.

Hendricks chuckled, raising his eyebrows at Brenda, whose sarcastic look in her friend's direction amused him greatly. "Well?" he asked. "Would you like to go? I've already arranged everything we'll need. Just have to pick the basket up after church."

Brenda looked excited, smiling wide. "I would love to go on a picnic with you and these two over here."

They all laughed at that.

CHURCH SERVICES WENT FASTER for Hendricks than ever before. The sermon was about Jesus speaking to his disciples about loving our fellow man and showing mercy. He enjoyed it and didn't feel sleepy even once throughout, which had often happened to him in the past.

He and his companions sat on the shore of the creek at the bottom of the hill on a blanket with the basket open in front of them. Jeremiah was stretched out on his side, looking up at Isabelle, feeding her strawberries.

"So, how long have you been here in Low Branch now?" he asked before taking a bite of his sandwich.

Brenda responded, her eyes on the pickle slice she was holding between her fingers. He thought it looked like she was suspicious of the pickle and didn't know if she really wanted to eat it.

"I guess it's been..." She looked at Isabelle.

"About six weeks, hasn't it been?" Isabelle answered for her.

"Yes, about that," Brenda responded with a nod.

"And do you like it?"

"I do like it very much. It's nice. The people here are nice. I haven't had any problems with anyone. It's very nice and peaceful, especially because my friend was so wonderful and generous in buying me the cottage. My own home. It's really so generous of him."

"You thanked me already," Jeremiah said. "No need to keep thanking me. You'll give me a big ego."

They laughed.

"I hope your time here gets nothing but better," Hendricks responded with a smile. He should have asked Brenda if she wanted to go on the picnic alone. He wouldn't be able to talk soberly to her with Jeremiah and Isabelle there.

But it would wait until the next time. And he would make sure there was one.

## 23

Hendricks didn't give up on the idea of telling Brenda everything he was feeling. By the time he woke up Monday morning, he was ready to go find her and tell all.

The boarding house was quiet and cool. He pulled on his shirt and buttoned it standing in front of the window, looking out. There were only a few people out in the street. He ran his eyes from one side of the street to the other, stopping only for a second on each person, thinking of a memory with them.

"Looks like it's going to be a slow day," he murmured, turning away from the window, topping off the shirt with the top button. He adjusted it as he walked back to the bed and sat on it to pull on his boots.

He didn't have any plans for the day. Denver should be in town at any minute. He'd sent the telegram letting his partner know which room he was in. He'd also informed Denver about his new fascination with the beautiful Brenda. So if he came back and found Denver sleeping in his room, it would be expected.

He left the room, feeling like if Denver was in town already, he would have gone to the saloon for breakfast and a beer or an early morning whiskey. Denver had a stomach like a steel trap. He could eat and drink anything any time of the day without being negatively affected.

Hendricks wasn't like that. He wouldn't be touching any wine, whiskey, or beer anytime soon. It hindered his functioning, something he didn't like. He didn't enjoy being out of control. It wasn't good for finding and capturing outlaws.

He used two fingers to salute the young lady behind the desk in the lobby of the boarding house. She smiled at him before returning her eyes to the open book on the desk in front of her.

The moment he stepped out of the building, he looked across the street and saw Brenda coming out of the flower shop. She was carrying a bouquet of fresh flowers, had them buried in her face, in fact. He thought he could see her breathing in deep from the way her shoulders drew up, and she closed her eyes.

His heart leaped into his throat when his eyes settled on her. He looked both ways before crossing over to where she was.

Hendricks was a little surprised by the look on her face when she saw him. She didn't look as happy as he would have liked. He could have sworn he saw a little fear in her features. What could she possibly be afraid of? Surely she wasn't afraid of him.

Regardless the look disappeared as quickly as it had come. It was replaced by a warm smile as she gazed at him.

"I've just picked out these flowers for the vase in my bedroom. What do you think of them?"

"I like them," he responded, dropping his eyes to the flowers she held in her hands directly in front of her chest. "They will look nice in your room, I'm sure. I only got a glance in, so unless you've changed it completely since I was there, I'd say those are a good choice."

Brenda tilted her head to the side. "Why, thank

you. How sweet of you to say. Would you like to walk me back to my house?"

Hendricks couldn't think of anything he would rather do. "I would love to. Thank you for asking me."

She was peculiarly quiet as they walked. He would have thought if she wanted him to walk with her, she might have something to say. He racked his brain for a topic. He shouldn't be expecting her to do all the talking, should he?

"I had a great time yesterday at the picnic. I hope we can do that again sometime. Maybe alone? I like your friend and his wife, but I would actually like to talk to you about something. I would like to see you more often. Socially, I mean. If I could maybe take you to dinner at the Side Street restaurant sometime?"

Brenda didn't say anything. She didn't look up at him either. The absence of the gesture made him nervous. Had he overstepped? Had he seen something that wasn't there?

"It's all right if you don't want to, I understand," he said quickly.

Brenda's eyes flipped up to him. He saw the sweetest look on her face but couldn't decipher what it meant.

"What is it?" he asked. "Please, tell me."

Brenda suddenly looked like she was going to cry. Her eyes darted away from him.

"Brenda?" He hoped he wasn't being too persistent. It was best, he thought, if everything was out in the open.

She stopped in the middle of the walk and turned to look up at him. Her eyes were so blue, so genuine and warm.

"I... I'm having a problem, Hendricks. And I don't know what to do about it."

"Talk to me. I'll help you, I promise. If there's anything I can do, I will."

"You can't help me. I don't think..." Her voice was so soft, he had to listen carefully, "but I'll tell you what it is." She started walking again. He remained by her side, his hands clasped behind his back as they strolled in the direction of her house.

"I'm listening," he said softly.

She pulled in a deep breath. "I made a decision before I met you to... to write to a man in another town. One of the marital arrangements, you know. Because of what my father did and trying to force me to marry Micah." She stopped speaking abruptly. When she continued, he could hear the emotion in her voice. "I don't know what to do, Hendricks. I've heard back from the man I wrote to, and his first letter... it seemed so insistent, and he said he wanted to come here to meet me."

The more she spoke, the worse Hendricks felt. He had competition he didn't even know about. She hadn't told him before about the letter she'd written. It wouldn't have made a difference to him if the man hadn't already written back with the notion that she was a free woman.

Which, of course, she was. Not that he wanted it that way. He wished he had the right to be jealous and get angry about it. But he couldn't be. It happened before they ever met.

"It's okay. You can just tell him to leave when he gets here, can't you?"

"I think he will recruit my father and force me to follow through with the original proposal. He also seemed the type to be very angry about this decision I've made."

Hendricks hoped he was right in thinking she was talking about a decision involving him.

"I don't want to marry the man, Hendricks." She sounded devastated. He stopped her walking, turned her to him, and pulled her into a hug.

"I'll help you through this, Brenda. Just ask me, just tell me what to do. I'm here for you."

## 24

The memory of his arms around her, his gentle hug, and the closeness of his body against her still swam through Brenda's mind the next day as she worked around her house. She'd cleaned thoroughly, getting up all the dust on her counters, even beating her curtains outside on the line.

She was hoping to see Hendricks today. She was going to town to help Isabelle in her shop anyway. She had to pay her friend back for all the kindness she'd shown. It was pulling up on noon before she was finished cleaning her house. She had also done her washing, putting her clean dresses on the line with the curtains.

Brenda had Hendricks on her mind when she

finished hanging her clothes up. She had to lift her arms and look up to put the things on the line. It reminded her of looking up at Hendricks. She could practically see him in front of her.

The house was so much brighter without the curtains hanging up. She could see all around her house from the outside. She didn't feel comfortable getting dressed in her room and did so quickly so she could leave the house. It wasn't until that moment she even realized how much she relied on simple curtains to make her feel safe.

Brenda stood at the door, smoothing down her dress right before she pulled the door open. In doing so, she almost ran into a large man standing on the other side.

He had a long dark brown mustache that reached down to his chin. The hair on his head was the same color, and he'd grown it out long and shaggy. She was immediately repulsed by the slovenly look he presented. She tried not to recoil visibly, but it was probably too late. If he was looking at her, he probably knew what she was thinking.

"H... Hello," she greeted him. "Can I help you?"

"Are you Brenda?" the man asked in a booming voice. He wasn't as tall as Hendricks. He was still tall, but most of his girth was in the width of his body.

And it wasn't all muscle. Brenda assumed there were muscles buried under the fat that made him rather rotund.

Other than his size and loud voice, he didn't really seem intimidating to Brenda.

"I am," she responded. It had to be Leonard. It had to be.

The man held out his hand to her. "Leonard Franklin," the man replied, holding out his hand and smiling wide. She couldn't help smiling back. "It is good to meet you finally. I'm sorry I didn't announce my arrival with a telegraph, but I didn't think of it before I left. I do hope you received my letter that I wanted to come to visit you first."

Brenda didn't know what to say. Her breath had caught in her throat. She hadn't written him back. In less than two weeks, he decided to make the trip to Low Branch. His town being so close had been one of the reasons why she'd chosen him. She hadn't thought about the fact that all he'd have to do was get on his horse and make the short trip to Low Branch.

"I did get your letter," she said, feeling stuck. She knew what she would have to do and didn't want to do it. "Please..." She stepped back from the door. "Do come in."

He walked past her, and she caught the scent of peppermint. It was pleasant and certainly smelled better than if he'd had a cigar clutched between his teeth.

He looked all around as he walked in, taking in her cottage as if he was thinking of buying it.

"What a lovely home you have for yourself here. Your friend bought it for you if I recall. I will have to make sure to sell it to the highest bidder so we make the most profit off of it."

Brenda had been hoping Leonard wouldn't come to Low Branch. She'd been hoping he would forget about her. When he'd come in her door, she'd wanted to be as pleasant as possible.

But when he immediately assumed he was taking all her possessions and selling them for profit, she knew there was no chance, even if he'd had one to begin with.

She wished Hendricks was there. It would have been perfect if he'd been visiting when Leonard showed up. She would have had more confidence to tell Leonard she'd changed her mind about the whole thing. As it was, she was a little frightened. Leonard was a stranger. A very large stranger. A man who could easily overpower her.

Was he determined enough to marry her that he would get violent?

Brenda's chest tightened with apprehension.

"I don't really want to sell my cottage," she said. "I think we should talk about this before any decisions are made."

"Darling, the decisions have already been made. I've got the pastor waiting and a ballroom for all my friends to come to after for a celebration like you've never seen before in your life. Let me tell you, little lady, you'll be real happy with me. I'll shower you with all the money and gifts you could want."

Brenda licked her lips and pressed them together. "That certainly sounds inviting, Mr. Frank—"

"Leonard. We're gonna be married. No reason to be formal, right?"

Brenda's heart ached. She wasn't going to marry this man. She had to make it clear. Should she wait until she had some form of protection? Or should she just forge ahead?

"Leonard, then." She blushed. "I have had a lot going on. Things have changed for me."

Leonard stopped for a moment, taking the time to study her closely. He was dressed in a fine suit. It was obvious, Brenda thought, that he had a lot of money. He was probably very powerful and pushed a lot of people around. Brenda had a sudden flashing thought that she would be thrust into the spotlight if Leonard decided to run for some kind of public office.

She shivered at the thought, covering it up by turning away from him. She said over her shoulder, "Would you like some coffee? Or something stronger?"

"I'd love a whiskey," he called out as if her house was massive and he had to yell to be heard. He laughed immediately afterward. "So sorry, didn't mean to yell at ya. I'm just used to it. Wait till you see my house. It's probably the biggest house you've ever seen. Though you told me about your father and what a tyrant he is. I'm sure you're used to the finer things. Honey, I'll give you all those fine things you're missing in your..." He snickered, looking around him, "your little shack here. I haven't been in a house this small since, well, I can't even remember. My folks raised me to have the best of everything. The luxuries, the staff, the food, the drink, the every-thing." He grinned at her. "Now you're gonna have those things. Aren't you excited?"

Brenda was struck into silence. Apparently, his wealth was as big as his ego. Still, no amount of money in this man's bank could sway her from the fact that she didn't have the one thing he would have wanted. Her heart. She'd already given that away.

Brenda didn't want to take it back from Hendricks, either. She wanted her bounty hunter.

25

A knock at the door made both of them swiftly turn to look at it. It was closed but not all the way. It was cracked. Four fingers slid around the edge.

Thoughts raced through Brenda's head. She hoped it was Hendricks coming to see her, even though that meant he would catch her with another man in her house. The two of them were alone. She would have some explaining to do.

But when the door was pushed open, she realized her mistake and felt her heart plummet into her stomach.

It was her father.

"Papa," she cried out. Her feelings were mixed. It was so nice to see him again. She hadn't missed him until she saw him at that moment. She'd only been angry at him for a short time and was more disappointed that he wouldn't listen to her than anything else. It was something she felt they would both eventually get over.

But she couldn't run to him and give him a hug as she wanted. He looked upset with her. She had to prepare herself for whatever lecturing he was about to give her. It wasn't going to change her mind, though. No matter what either had to say to the other.

He stood there for a moment before sliding his eyes to Leonard.

"Is this a visitor?" he asked, not greeting her back. She could tell he was as disappointed in her as she was in him. But she felt justified. He was trying to run her life. Not the other way around.

"Yes. I have been looking for someone to marry instead of Micah. He doesn't want to marry me, Father." She knew he hated it when she called him Father instead of Papa, which he preferred.

"I know he doesn't." He just rolled his eyes. "He has told us repeatedly every day since you left. I have come to accept it isn't going to happen. You are a grown woman and chose to run away from me rather than marry your own best friend. That must mean something, and like I keep telling Michael, I didn't raise a foolish girl. You have your reasons for everything you do."

Brenda tilted her head to the side, giving him a gentle look of love. "You won't force me to marry Micah now?"

Her father shook his head. "No. I've given up. You've won."

"Oh, Papa!" Brenda ran across the room and threw her arms around his neck. "Thank you, thank you. I'm so glad."

She could hear his smile in his voice. It was nice to have his arms around her again. She'd never felt so safe as a little girl as when she was in his arms.

"So you will come home now? Or will you be moving to this young man's home?"

Brenda released him from her grip and took a step back. She glanced at Leonard with regret in her eyes. "I'm sorry. I was supposed to. This is Leonard Franklin, Papa. He's the man I wrote to when I was contemplating marriage through a magazine. But I've changed my mind."

She said the last sentence almost directly to Leonard, trying to use a gentle voice. He raised his eyebrows to her, giving her a surprised look that was reflected on her father's face.

"I have a lot to offer you, Miss Brenda," the man said, his voice loud in her little home. It made her cringe. She hoped he didn't see her reaction. She wasn't trying to hurt his feelings. "I think your father would agree once he hears who I am."

"I would love to know who you are, sir," Brenda's father interjected, stepping forward with his hand out. "I need to know the name of my daughter's new suitor."

Brenda wanted to scream out that he wasn't her suitor, that there was only one man she was going to marry, and he wasn't in the room.

She said nothing.

Leonard went to her father, taking his hand. "Leonard Franklin. Good to meet you, sir. I am a wealthy man with a ranch I live on and another I rent out to a family from Germany. I own several businesses, and they are all in very good standing. Your daughter will be very well taken care of."

"I can take care of myself." The words blurted out of her mouth before she could stop them."

Leonard glanced at her, obvious amusement on his face. "Oh, I'm sure you can, my dear." He seemed to dismiss her then, turning to her father with one arm stretched out, so his hand rested on the older man's shoulder. "I'm stayin' in town at the boarding house. What say we go and have a talk, sir?"

"But I don't want to—"

For the second time in her life, her father turned his back, his mind distracted by the prospect of further financial gain.

"Chuck Watson. And that sounds like a grand idea. Good to meet you, too." He gave Brenda another moment of attention when he looked at her and said, "You were smart to invite this man to come to see you. We will be back later with plans. Good thinking, Brenda."

Brenda was positive he'd heard her protests and decided to ignore them. She followed as they walked to the door.

"But, Papa, I don't want to marry Leonard. I have an—"

"You'll change your mind, my dear," Leonard cut in, his huge grin actually genuine-looking.

Brenda hated the fact that she was certain he meant well. It should matter, but he really did. He had responded to the letter she'd sent in response to his ad. She didn't need to write the letter. She herself had caused all the problems she was suffering with now.

When she was done feeling sorry for herself, she

called out behind them as they mounted their horses, "I have another man I want to marry, do you hear?"

Her father was the one to react to those words. He was already in the saddle, so he pulled the horse up to the steps at the end of the porch.

"Who is this other man?"

"He owns a ranch, too. He's the one I've been seeing since I was introduced to him. Socially. I can't and won't marry someone else."

"I was thinking about buying an island near the coast of England," Leonard remarked casually, his eyes on Brenda. "Don't you want that? Isn't that something you can only imagine? I can give it to you. You've never traveled, have you? I don't mean between these little towns in Texas. I mean across the seas on a tremendous boat. I mean across the nation from coast to coast, seeing the beauty that is our country. Don't you want those things?"

Brenda didn't know how to explain to a man like him how little material things meant to her.

"I would love to see those things," she said, "but not at the expense of my heart."

Her words seemed to fall on deaf ears. The two men looked at each other, her father's face curious, Leonard's face confused.

He shook his head, furrowing his brow. "You will change her mind," he said firmly as if he could will such a thing into action. He moved his eyes to her father. "She will change her mind. Let's go. Let her think about this for a bit."

Brenda watched them leave, dread filling her from head to toe.

**26**

___

Hendricks was sitting back in his chair, pushing it off the front legs, nursing the glass of beer he had his hand wrapped around. He let his eyes wander around the room, eyeing everyone there, not exactly suspiciously, more curiously.

"How you doin' today, Hendricks?" He heard from behind him. He turned to see the sheriff had come in and walked directly toward him.

"Not too bad, Carl. How about you?"

"I ain't complaining," the older man replied. "Just thought I'd step in for a beer. Just got off my shift and Deputy Caldwell is in charge. He knows what he's doing. The town is safe with him lookin' out for us."

"That's good to hear," Hendricks said, grinning. "I feel reassured. I haven't seen Kelsey anywhere yet." He wasn't going to tell the sheriff he'd been completely preoccupied with something else. A beautiful woman. "You heard anything?"

"Nope. You think he's moved on?"

Hendricks thought about it. He'd only been in Low Branch for just over a week. Just because he hadn't seen Kelsey didn't mean the man wasn't hiding out. The outlaw was likely to suspect Hendricks was in Low Branch, and judging by the way things had ended the last time, Hendricks suspected Kelsey—true to form—would be keeping low, in the shadows, watching him.

"I don't know. I doubt it. When he's got a bee in his bonnet, he tends to go after whoever or whatever he wants relentlessly. He just takes his time. He's a sloth."

Sheriff Bancroft gestured to the barkeep, who nodded at him. He slid into the chair next to Hendricks, yanking it out and plopping down with a big sigh. "Sloth, huh?" He shook his head. "I don't like the sound of that. He's real elusive. Hard to track down. Pops up like a jumpin' spider."

The swinging doors at the front of the saloon allowed a bright stream of sunlight in. When it was blocked, Hendricks moved his eyes to see who was coming in and was on his feet a second later.

"Denver!" He held up his hand to show Denver where he was. He was glad to see his partner after such a long absence. It had been nearly a month since the two of them split up.

His partner made his way through the growing crowd, coming straight over. They shook hands, and Denver pulled his partner into a man hug, pounding him on the back.

"Good to see you, partner," Denver said loudly. "Good to see you."

"It's good to see you, too. I figgered you'd be showin' your face sooner or later." Hendricks turned to the sheriff. "This here's my partner, Denver Jackson. Denver, this is Sheriff Carl Bancroft. He's been keepin' an eye out for Kelsey. Got his deputies on it, too. So far, no sightings."

"He's real good at staying hidden until he's ready to come out," Denver remarked, shaking hands with the sheriff before sitting. He was about the same height as the sheriff but not nearly as round.

"I've got a beer coming," the sheriff said. "You want one?"

"I think I'll be gettin' somethin' a little stronger

than that," Denver replied, getting to his feet again and crossing to the bar.

"How long you two been partners?" the sheriff asked. Hendricks looked at the lawman when he answered.

"Long time. Real long time."

"You're a lot younger than him. I guess he's taught you everything he knows, is that right?"

"I reckon," Hendricks replied. He'd been a bounty hunter for so long that it was hard to remember he was only twenty-nine years old. He'd caught many outlaws since he was a teen just starting out. "He's taught me a lot."

"Don't let him fool ya." Denver leaned on the corner of the bar, waiting for the barkeep to pay attention to him. He turned his head toward the two men. "He's got the talent." He tapped himself on the nose. "Just seems like he knows where they are without having to put in any effort. I've wondered where he gets his information sometimes. Then it comes out that he's just guessing. He just happens to guess right all the time."

Hendricks chuckled, shaking his head. He rocked on the back two legs of the chair, crossing his arms over his chest. He was flattered and couldn't help showing it.

"Look at him. He's blushing."

Hendricks was a little annoyed that his friend was teasing him so loudly. He didn't want the entire town to see him blushing. And it felt like the whole town was there in the saloon.

Sheriff Bancroft leaned over and patted him on the back.

"You'll be all right," he said consolingly. Hendricks looked to see he had a teasing grin on his face. He couldn't help grinning back.

"Yeah, okay, okay."

Hendricks wondered if Denver showing up would bring Kelsey out of the woodwork or drive him further away. He felt more secure with his partner being in town. The likelihood of Kelsey showing his face with the two of them there wasn't very high. He didn't know how to feel about that. It was like they were giving up on the outlaw.

It wasn't Denver who was giving up on it, though, and Hendricks knew it. He was straying away from his chosen career because of a woman. He was getting close to wanting a major change, a change that meant he wouldn't be going out into dangerous situations, getting shot, and having to put up with the pain for months. He'd grown used to ignoring the ache in his side. In fact, he had begun to associate the reminder with being in the pretty little cottage belonging to the woman who had taken his heart.

"Hendricks." Denver was back at the table, snapping his fingers in front of Hendricks's eyes. "You there, buddy? You there?"

Hendricks laughed. "Yeah. Just thinking."

"Thinkin' about that little lady, huh?" Sheriff Bancroft asked, winking at Hendricks, further causing his cheeks to flame up. He wished he could control that reaction. He looked away, casting his eyes in the direction of the barkeep, who wasn't looking at him. He concentrated on the man, even though his mind was wandering, pondering where Brenda could be at that moment.

"Yeah," he said. "I reckon I am. So?"

He wasn't really being confrontational. The smile on his face gave that away. The sheriff shook his head.

"I figure you'll be in with that girl pretty quick," the sheriff said, tapping one finger on the table distractedly. "I've seen the way she looks at ya. She's in love with ya."

Those were the words Hendricks wanted to hear. It thrilled him that a stranger had noticed.

"I don't know a lot about Brenda," the sheriff

continued as Denver came back and sat from the bar and sat down, "but I know Jeremiah, and he's had a few discussions with me about what her pa was doing to her, tryin' to make her marry that boy. She'll be a lot happier with you, I'm sure. A lot happier."

## 27

Isabelle looked up from the soil she was sifting through. "Look at this little gem I found in this dirt, Brenda," she said, holding up a bright red, shiny gem. "Isn't it beautiful?"

"It's gorgeous." Brenda tried to show a lot of excitement as her friend wanted her to, but her heart wasn't in it.

Isabelle stopped what she was doing, gazing at her friend with concerned eyes. "What's going on, Brenda? Are you all right?"

"He came to my house," Brenda said. "I went to the door and opened it, and there he stood."

Isabelle blinked at her. After a moment, she lifted her eyebrows. "Hendricks?"

Brenda's heart reacted to his name, but she

shook her head, not feeling any better. In fact, it made her feel worse. "Leonard. The man I wrote to. I'm so disappointed. I wish I had never written to him. I don't know what to do."

Brenda threw herself onto the tall stool, leaning forward to put her head in her hands, her elbows on the table in front of her.

Isabelle grabbed her hand and squeezed it between both of hers. "Oh no. He just came to your house? Without sending you a message first?"

Brenda shook her head. "I suppose he thought his letter was the warning. I should have known since his town is so close to Low Branch. That's why I chose him. Remember?"

Isabelle nodded. "Yes, I remember," she said. "I encouraged you, too. I'm so sorry, honey. I didn't know you were going to fall in love with a wounded bounty hunter instead."

Brenda liked the sound of that. She turned her head slightly and gave her friend a warm smile, though it was small. "I do love him, Isabelle. I truly do. I have to tell him. I have to make Leonard and my father understand."

"Well, what was he like? Are you afraid of him? Does he seem as intimidating as he sounded in the letter?"

Brenda thought about it. She pictured him in her mind. He wasn't as frightening as he could have been. She shook her head, looking for the right words to describe him.

"He's physically tall, but he didn't frighten me. He was actually kind of jolly. He is very confident. I suppose that's because he has a lot of money. He boasted about it. And then my father showed up and—"

"Your father showed up?" Isabelle's voice was two octaves higher than usual, and her eyebrows shot up in surprise. "What is he doing here? He didn't let you know he was coming, did he?"

Brenda shook her head. "And do you know what he said to me? He said that he no longer wanted me to marry Micah and that he understood. But Micah's pa is still adamant about it. Regardless, Pa doesn't care if I don't marry Micah, but now he's determined to have me marry Leonard. It feels like he thinks I'm a property instead of his own daughter."

Isabelle tilted her head, sympathy in her eyes. "Oh no. That seems like such a coincidence that your father would show up at the same time as Leonard. Do you think they've been in contact?"

Brenda hadn't thought about that. She'd been in such shock that Leonard showed up out of the blue and then to have her father concede and tell her he wouldn't insist on the arranged marriage to Micah. She hadn't put two and two together.

"Oh Lord," she whispered, tingling at the thought that she might have figured out what happened. "Leonard must have done some searching to find my father. Unless he already knew Papa. But what are the real chances of them showing up at the same time? They pretended not to know each other, but really, they must, mustn't they?"

"I think they must," Isabelle replied softly, "but I don't really know, do I? I just don't see them showing up at the same time. It's too much of a coincidence."

"Leonard doesn't seem like a bad man. If I was interested in a man for his money or if I wasn't already in love with someone else, I would marry him. He's not bad looking. I don't get the feeling he would be violent with me."

She relaxed a little, sitting back in the chair. It seemed only logical that her father and Leonard had gotten in touch somehow.

"Where is Hendricks now?" Isabelle asked.

"I haven't seen him since I came into town. As soon as Leonard and Papa left, I got my shoes on and followed them into town. I saw them go to the saloon, and maybe that's where they still are. I don't know."

"You should go find Hendricks," Isabelle urged her. "Talk to him. You need to make sure he knows which side you're on. Did you tell him about Leonard? I mean that you wrote to him? Does he know about that?"

Brenda nodded, feeling tears rising to her eyes, clogging her throat. "I had to tell him. He met me yesterday and walked home with me, and I told him. He didn't seem bothered. He told me it would all work out. I know it will. I can fix it. I have to. "

Isabelle put one arm around Brenda's shoulders and squeezed her warmly. "I'm so sorry you have to go through this. I wish your father had understood before he was approached by someone with more money and clout than Micah. I can only think that must be why he is doing this. Didn't you say his best friend is Micah's pa?"

"Yeah, that's right."

Isabelle nodded. "I don't want to speak ill of someone I don't know. But Jeremiah has told me about a few things he's heard or experienced with your father. And he is a man who sees the dollar sign in front of his eyes wherever he goes. I don't want to hurt your feelings, Brenda. That's just what Jeremiah has noticed and heard, that's all."

Brenda shook her head. "I know, Isabelle. I've always known that the one thing my father loves more than anything else—including me—is money. He'll do anything for wealth and power."

"Include marry off his daughter like cattle." Isabelle's voice had suddenly dropped low. Brenda could tell the subject annoyed the woman.

"I love him," she murmured quietly. "I just can't do what he wants me to do anymore. Now that Hendricks is in my life, I don't want another man and won't marry another man. When Papa finds out Hendricks is a bounty hunter with no money, he won't be happy. He won't encourage it or bless us when we get married."

"You'll figure this out," Isabelle said. "Me and Jeremiah and Hendricks, we'll all help you. Your father won't be happy, maybe, but he can't stop you. Hendricks is highly respected. People like him. He's a gentleman, and he will protect you at all costs. That's something this... Leonard... doesn't sound like something he would do. He sounds as money-hungry as your father. I'll just bet they're in the saloon making plans that have to do with business and not a wedding."

The thought made Brenda chuckle. "Of course they aren't talking about a wedding. That's for you and me to do." She took in a deep breath, forcing herself to relax. "And it won't be to Leonard. You're right. Hendricks will figure this out."

**28**

———

Hendricks looked up when the light coming into the saloon was blocked again. Two strangers came in. Most of the people in Low Branch were strangers, though, so it didn't mean anything to him. Neither of them was Kelsey, so it didn't much matter to him who they were.

They took a table near the three men. Hendricks wouldn't have given them another thought if the younger one hadn't immediately started talking about a woman named Brenda. Could there be another Brenda nearby? Nah, had to be *his* Brenda.

"You think Brenda's gonna change her mind?" he asked.

Hendricks struggled not to jerk his head in their

direction. The sheriff, however, did move his eyes to them and stared at the two men, his gaze unwavering.

"I have no idea whether she will or not," the older man said, shaking his head. "It doesn't really matter. She's gonna have to get married. She's gonna be old and gray if she keeps turning men down. Somethin' wrong with her maybe."

"Nah, nothin' wrong with that daughter of yours," the younger one said.

Chills ran from Hendricks's neck down his spine. That was Brenda's father? He wondered if the men had confronted Brenda. Immediate worry slipped through him. He balled up his fist to keep himself under control. He focused on Denver, who was also listening and had quickly figured out what was going on. He didn't say a word and returned Hendricks's gaze without a word. All three men stayed quiet while Brenda's father and the other man continued talking.

"She just doesn't know what's good for her," the younger man said vehemently. "I can take good care of her. She's never gonna have to worry about a thing. It will be good business for both you and me. And for her, of course. For us all."

"You don't know how often I've tried to tell her

that. She's just a woman. She doesn't understand these things. You and I know what's best for her. She doesn't want to grow old alone and lonely. She needs a man in her life. That boy…" Brenda's father shook his head. "He doesn't see that he's hurting her and not helping her. He's keepin' her from findin' what she needs."

"That's when you bring the gander to the goose," the younger man said loudly and boisterously. "Barkeep. I'll have a beer. And one for my friend." He roared the words overtop the hum of the room. No one stopped talking. They just continued on with what they were doing.

Everyone except Hendricks. How much longer he could keep himself under control was a mystery. If he had to hazard a guess, it wouldn't be much longer.

"Hard to believe ya tracked me down," Brenda's father said, grinning from ear to ear. "You really wanted to find her, didn't you?"

"Oh, I knew where she lived," the younger man replied, shaking his head, his large arms crossed over his chest. Hendricks had to admit he was impressed with the suit the man was wearing. "She's the one who wrote to me, remember?"

Hendricks caught the look both the sheriff and

Denver sent in his direction. He couldn't tell them he knew already, so he shook his head at them. Denver understood that it wasn't important or a surprise to Hendricks, probably because they'd been partners for over a decade. He knew Hendricks well. If it wasn't important to him, it wasn't important to Denver.

"That's why I don't understand why she was acting that way today," Mr. Watson said, shaking his head. "She wrote to you. Shouldn't she be happy to see you? She outright said she didn't want to get married now. Well, no daughter of mine is gonna go through her life without a man because she thinks she has to. She wrote to you. She just doesn't understand how much being married will give her a new life. She wants children. I know she does. She can't have children without getting married. Need a man for somethin' like that."

"Yeap. I agree with ya. It's for her own good. Gonna sell that little cottage, too. I'm sure you can find someone who wants it, can't you? You got contacts here?"

It hurt Hendricks's heart to hear they planned to sell the cottage. He was aware of how much Brenda loved it. He couldn't take it any longer. He spun in his chair and stared at the two men.

"You're talking about Brenda Watson, aren't you?" he asked in a gruff voice.

Both men froze, gazing back at him.

"Who are you?" the younger one asked, in a voice that was neither confrontational nor friendly.

"My name is Hendricks Potter. I'm the one your daughter is going to marry, Mr. Watson. Me. We are in love with each other." He said the words hoping beyond hope he was right about how she felt about him. "If you want to know why she was acting that way today, it was because I am the one who will marry her. I love her. I won't treat her like cattle. Something to be bought and sold like property."

He was somewhat surprised by the reaction of the younger man, who must have been the one Brenda had told him about. But this man, though he looked wealthy, didn't look scary or intimidating. He wasn't as tall or muscular as Hendricks, but a fist fight wasn't really something he would expect from the man sitting at the other table. He looked like a negotiator, a talker, not a fighter.

"Well, well, well..." he finally said, turning his eyes to his companion. "What say you, Chuck? Did you know about this man before we got here today? Didn't tell me about him?"

Hendricks answered for Brenda's father before

the older man could say anything. "I didn't inform Mr. Watson about my love for his daughter, and I'm quite sure she hasn't mentioned it to him. She says he is very focused on marrying her to a man with a lot of money. I don't have a lot of money. I'm a bounty hunter, and I'm thinking of giving up the job to stay here in Low Branch."

"I'll be offering him a deputy position," the sheriff said, cutting in to add the remark.

Hendricks tried to continue on seamlessly as if he already knew the sheriff was going to offer him a position. The news, though, made his body light up in flames of anticipation. It was the perfect resolution to his problem. He could give up the road, not go back to the dangerous job he'd been doing for so long. Low Branch was a small community that hadn't seen any crime since Hendricks arrived. It was peaceful, just the right place to raise a family with Brenda.

"You can't come here and just take her away without remembering that she's made friends and ties here that you can't just sever and think it's for her own good. She's twenty-one years old. She needs to make her own decisions. Especially when it comes to a decision that will affect the rest of her life."

Leonard pulled in a deep breath through his nose. He cast his eyes outward, looking at the other patrons in the saloon. None of them were paying any attention, busy with their own lives.

Hendricks waited with bated breath for what he would say next. He had to know Hendricks could beat him into the ground if he had to. And for Brenda, there was a good chance he would do just that.

## 29

_______________

Brenda left the garden shop and walked in the direction of her cottage. She hadn't brought her horse to town and was now wishing she had. It would have cut the walk down to just five minutes on horseback. As it was, she would have to walk for twenty to get home.

Good thing it was a pleasant day. The sun was shining above her head, but a cool breeze kept her from getting too hot. She hadn't brought a parasol, but she rarely used one. She was used to the Texas weather. She was new to Low Branch, not the environment.

She couldn't help thinking about her father and Leonard showing up at the same time. How was that possible? It seemed only logical that they had come at the same time. They had gotten to know each other first through correspondence, most likely. Brenda was sure she'd never seen Leonard at her house or in town doing business with her father.

Her mind strayed to the man she really wanted to think about. No matter what she was doing, it was Hendricks who was always in the back of her mind. She preferred thinking about him more than anyone or anything else right now.

She was hoping Hendricks would come by that evening and see her. She wanted to explain to him like Isabelle had said to do before he found out some other way.

As she walked, she watched for him but didn't see him. She got all the way to her cottage and was inside without even spotting his horse. She could have gone in search of him, but she was afraid she would run into Leonard and her father in town. That would only prove to destroy her reputation even further. If people knew she'd answered Leonard's ad and saw how extremely wealthy he was, she wouldn't stand a chance against the rumors and degradation. She wasn't that kind of woman. If she was forced to marry Leonard, as nice as he seemed to be, she would forever be known as a gold-digging woman, someone who would do anything just for the almighty dollar.

Even if he was the richest man in the world, Brenda knew she would be miserable with him. She would forever be thinking about Hendricks, wondering what he was doing and where he was. If he was still alive and well.

She couldn't imagine having to tell him she couldn't see him anymore, that they would never have the one-on-one picnic he'd asked her for. The thought of never seeing him again made her entire body ache.

She couldn't allow it to stand. She had to make sure her father and Leonard let her be, free to live her own life. With Hendricks.

She had taken off her shoes and was in the kitchen making tea when she heard a knock on her door. Her heart raced, wondering who it was. Had Leonard and her father come back? Or was it Hendricks?

She pulled in a deep, calming breath and went to the door, smoothing her dress down and patting her hair to make sure it wasn't wild all over her head.

Brenda put her hand on the knob and tried once more to settle her pounding heart. She opened the door and found herself staring into the eyes of a stranger. Her eyebrows went up and then furrowed.

"Can I help you?" she asked.

"You've had a visitor lately," the man said in a menacing way.

Frightened chills erupted over Brenda's body. She stepped back quickly and threw the door closed. Before it could, the man jutted out one hand to stop it, knocking it back against her. She fell back to get out of the way, crying out.

"You've had a visitor lately," the man repeated, towering over her, stepping into the cottage, and throwing the door closed behind him.

"No... no, I don't know what you're talking about. You... Who are you... what do you want..." She backed away from him, still on the ground, crawling like a crab. He only took two steps to be right beside her, reaching down and balling up the front of her dress in his hands. He lifted her as if she weighed no more than a feather.

"I don't like your visitor," the man continued, staring into her eyes with his black ones. Even if they hadn't been black, that was the way she would have seen him. She was trembling, and tears were streaking down her cheeks.

"Please. I don't know what you mean. I don't know who you're talking about."

The man brought her face close to his, jerking her dress so that she thought it might rip. She didn't want herself exposed to the world, much less this horrible, frightening man.

"We're just gonna wait here until he gets back here." She could smell whiskey and cigarettes on his breath. She turned her face away, recoiling from the disgusting odor. "And you're gonna make me some of that coffee you was making."

"I'm making tea," Brenda replied, swallowing hard. "I mean... I was making tea. I can start some coffee... if you want." Fear was making it hard for her to breathe and speak. "I don't mind... really, I don't." Maybe placating the man would keep him from hurting her. So far, he hadn't done any more than manhandle her. But he looked on edge. He looked like he could snap at any moment. She had no doubt if he snapped, he would kill her.

"You make me coffee." He shoved her toward the kitchen, pulling one of the guns from the holsters at his side and shoving it into her ribs. "Go now. I want some coffee. I'm dead tired, and I gotta be on my feet when the bounty hunter gets here. He's coming, and I'm gonna be here waiting for him."

"He's... I don't know if he's coming." She spoke shakily but moved away from the barrel of the gun toward the kitchen. It wasn't comfortable poking against her. She couldn't feel how cold it was through her dress, but she still imagined it was cold as ice. When he jabbed her with it, she felt like it was a knife.

"Make the coffee," he directed. He took a seat at the small kitchen table, staring at her, the gun still aimed at her as she went about the business of making coffee. She glanced over her shoulder at him.

"Do you mind if I make a cup of tea for myself? It's been brewing and—"

"I don't care what you do," the man replied. She guessed at that moment it had to be Kelsey Bradshaw. What other man would be pursuing Hendricks and would know about her?

"Th... thank you." She turned back, running her eyes over the ingredients lined up on the shelf above the stove to the right. There was nothing she could put in the coffee to make him sleepy. They were all spices and a few herbs. Nothing useful at all.

She poured the tea into a cup and set the pan back on the stove, away from the hot burner. The fresh pot of water for the coffee was put in its place.

Brenda took a sip of her tea, turning to look at the man at her table. He was dirty from head to toe, his hair greasy, his face smeared, his clothes reeking of grime and age. She was surprised since he was a notorious outlaw who had robbed banks, trains, stagecoaches, and individuals. She didn't know a lot about him, but she did know he had amassed a lot of money at that point. Where could it have all gone? It wasn't going to the clothes on his back. That was a fact.

"You are Kelsey Bradshaw, aren't you?" she asked, doing her best not to show how frightened she was. She couldn't stop her hands from shaking, though. He would just have to see that. There was nothing she could do.

He sneered, giving her an appreciative nod. "Yeah, that's me. How'd ya guess? Never mind that, let me." He lifted the gun and gestured at her with it. "He's said somethin' about me, eh? Talkin' about his prey with his little woman, eh?"

He didn't tell me a lot about you," she responded hotly. "In fact, he hardly mentioned you at all. We've been too busy getting to know each other to let a creature like you get in between us."

Kelsey was on his feet a second later, approaching her and putting the barrel of the gun against her cheek, running it up and down lightly. "You really want to talk that way, little lady?" he asked in a low voice.

She didn't respond. Her voice had caught in her throat, and her heart almost stopped beating from fear. She shook her head silently.

He grinned. "Say yer sorry."

Her heart slammed in her chest. She stared into his eyes, unwilling to say the words. She forced them out reluctantly. "I'm... sorry..." she whispered.

He let out one chuckle deep in his throat. "Sure you are."

**30**

———

"Well, I didn't expect that," the stranger said. He pushed his chair back as he leaned forward, his hand stretched out to Hendricks. "Leonard Franklin. I'm not a man who is gonna step on another man's toes. I'm not one to fight, especially when it looks like my competition is a lawman."

Brenda's father was staring at Leonard with surprise. "You're just gonna give up like that?"

Leonard sat back after shaking Hendricks's hand. "I don't know what you mean, Chuck. That girl has a right to love who she wants. I'm not gonna take her away if it's gonna make her miserable. I'm a gentleman. I'm a man with a great deal of wealth and power. I don't need to force a woman to marry me."

The barkeep brought over the beer for the men. None of them spoke while he set them down. When he walked away, Hendricks had a thought.

"Can I ask ya somethin'?" Hendricks asked in a curious voice.

Leonard gave him a wide-eyed look. "What you want to know?" he asked.

"If you have all this wealth and power, why did you put an ad out to find a wife?"

Leonard let out a belly laugh, sitting forward with one arm resting on the table next to him. He had Hendricks's attention fully. A glance at the other men would tell him they were paying attention. This was a man who demanded it, just by his very presence. At the same time, Hendricks didn't get a bad feeling from him and was truly interested and curious.

"I'll tell ya the deal, son." The term made Hendricks chuckle inside. Leonard probably wasn't that much older than him. "When you look like this," He swept one hand from his head to his toes, following his body, "and ya have the kind of money I've got in the bank, you gotta be careful about everything. You gotta be careful who you do business with, who you share you're life with, everything. You can't be too careful, as a matter of fact. So when the dear Miss Brenda wrote to me, I had my people track down her family. I have to know who I'm dealing with, don't I? Putting the ad in was the best way I could think of to find a woman who would appreciate me for who I am instead of what I've got."

From what Hendricks had heard so far, it would be impossible for Brenda, or any other woman who wrote to Leonard, to know exactly what they were getting themselves into after meeting him. He should have stuck to letters.

"I didn't know she already had a man," Leonard continued, a big grin on his open face. Hendricks doubted there was ever a need for this man to lie about anything. He would probably tell the truth no matter how harsh it was. And politely at that.

A charming man. Hendricks didn't doubt he had his choice of women.

"I'm not gonna take your woman," Leonard said when Hendricks didn't respond. "I'm not that kind of man."

Hendricks stared at the man.

"I think we should go see her," he said. "We should all three of us talk to her. Let her know everything will be all right. As long as you aren't gonna make her marry Micah." He moved his eyes to Leonard. "Or this charming gentleman right here."

Leonard let out a happy chuckle. "Thanks," he said loudly. "I think it would be grand to go see her and sort all this out. Maybe if ya both play your cards right, I'll pay for a grand wedding for ya."

Hendricks grinned. "You gotta tell that to Brenda. She's the one who's gonna want to know that. She and Isabelle. Be careful. They might just drain your bank account." He didn't know or really think the ladies would do that. Brenda definitely didn't strike him as the materialistic or greedy type.

"Let's get on out there, then. You know where the cottage is?" Hendricks asked the question before he remembered they had been talking like they had already spoken with her.

"We were there this morning," Leonard responded, pushing to his feet, seemingly not bothered at all by the question. "She was a little upset when we left, wasn't she, Chuck? I reckon we should have tried to find out why."

Brenda's father snorted. "I know why she was upset. She doesn't like to be told what to do. She's always been that way. An independent thinker for a woman." He shook his head.

"I'm gonna stay here and mind the saloon," the sheriff said, lifting his beer glass in the air. "You all go do what you need to do. You ain't gonna need me."

Hendricks nodded at the man. "Yeah, you stay here and make sure you watch for Kelsey. He's still lurkin' about somewhere, I'm sure of it." He looked at Denver. "You wanna stay here, too? You don't even know Brenda. She probably won't be as comfortable if a complete stranger is in the room." He glanced over his shoulder at Leonard, who was standing with his hands on his hips and a wide grin plastered to his face. "A man not involved in this anyway."

"Nah, let him come along," Leonard said in a friendly way, sliding one hand in front of him as if he was wiping away Hendricks's idea, dismissing it. "The more, the merrier, right?"

Hendricks shrugged, grinning at the other man. "Sure, I reckon." He looked at Denver. "Well. Let's go. What are you waiting for?"

**31**

———

Hendricks stepped up to Brenda's door and lifted his hand to knock.

After doing so, he turned to his left and his right, looking at the other men, who were just behind him.

"This is gonna come as a real surprise to her," he said, grinning wide. "She's probably gonna faint from the shock of seeing us all together."

The men laughed appreciatively, nodding.

They waited, and when the door was finally opened, Brenda only pulled it enough to look out at them. As he expected, Brenda's eyes widened, and she swept them from one man to another.

"What's going on?" she whispered.

"We wanted to come in and talk to you, Brenda,"

Hendricks responded happily. He couldn't wait to tell her everything had been worked out. But she wouldn't open the door further, even though he had leaned in to go in. She didn't step to the side, either. He gazed at her, enjoying the beauty of her face. "Are you all right?" he asked softly.

She blinked rapidly. He noticed tears had come to her eyes as they stood there. He shook his head, holding out both hands. "It's okay, Brenda. Everything's been worked out. We can do whatever we want. We can get married whenever you want."

Brenda's eyes widened even further, and the tears came pouring out, streaming down her cheeks. She sucked her breath in and let it out again. "I... I..."

Hendricks was stunned when she was suddenly jerked backward. She hadn't stepped back. She had been pulled back. Her arms and head fell forward as she was pulled. In her place a moment later was a face he would never have expected to see.

It was Kelsey Bradshaw.

His face crumpled into a rage, and he balled up his fists.

Kelsey had not expected to see the other three men with Hendricks. It was obvious by the look on his face. He'd thought he would only need to shoot

Hendricks and Brenda and run off, free as a bird once again.

Before Hendricks or any of the other men could react, Kelsey took the gun in his hand and rammed it into Hendricks's wounded side. Though the injury had healed quite a lot, it was still incredibly sore. It hadn't been long enough for it to have completely healed at that point.

Pain shot through Hendricks like he'd been shot all over again. He heard Brenda scream, but it was muffled by his own outcry. He doubled over and felt his companions moving past him quickly. It was Brenda who came out of the house seconds later.

"He's run through the house to the back," she cried out. "You can catch him if one of you is faster. Please get him."

Rage spilled through Hendricks. He grabbed Brenda's hand and raced past her, pulling her back into the house. "Go to your room and stay there, Brenda," he demanded. "I don't want you getting hurt. You can't come with us."

"Stay with me," Brenda pleaded with him. He was tempted. He never wanted to leave her again.

But this was one quest he couldn't leave to her father, a stranger, and his partner. He had to take care of Kelsey or at least be involved in the arrest.

He let go of her hand, grabbed the back of her head, and pulled her into a quick passionate kiss. He enjoyed the stunned look on her face when he let her go.

"I'll be right back," he vowed.

He ran out the back door and chased after the men in the distance. He caught up to Brenda's father, who was panting hard.

"Let us do this," he said, grabbing the man's arm without slowing his pace. "Go back to her. She needs to be with someone."

Chuck immediately stopped running, his arm jerking out of Hendricks's when he did so.

Hendricks heard when the two men ahead of him tackled Kelsey. He could hear the enraged cries of the outlaw as he fought for his life. Several gunshots went off right when Hendricks came into a clearing where his partner and the wealthy stranger were fighting the outlaw. It looked to Hendricks like Leonard was concentrating on attempting to grab the gun out of Kelsey's hand while Denver was trying to wrestle the outlaw to the ground.

Kelsey was fighting with everything he had.

When Hendricks got in the fight, it was over quickly. On his own, Hendricks was just bigger. Kelsey was fast on his feet, a quick draw and a hard puncher. It seemed three men was the trick to catch the sneaky fighter.

In a whirlwind of motion, Leonard jerked the gun from Kelsey's hand, and another shot went off. Denver's arms were tight around Kelsey's chest, and he jerked the man to the side, tossing him away. Hendricks was on him a second later, literally sitting on Kelsey's chest. He balled up his fist and punched the outlaw as hard as he could on the side of the head.

Kelsey's eyes closed, and he ceased moving.

Hendricks jumped up from the man, his eyes on Kelsey's chest. When it continued to rise and fall, he knew the punch hadn't killed him.

"Okay, he's out," he said. "Leonard, run back to the saloon and get the sheriff. Or fetch a deputy on the way if you see one. Send 'em back here."

"Yep." The man bolted back toward the house.

"Stop and let Brenda and Chuck know what happened," Hendricks yelled out. As he continued running, the man in the suit and tie lifted one hand up in the air to acknowledge what he'd heard. Hendricks turned his eyes to Denver. "I think there's some rope in that shed over there. You want to get it? We'll hog tie him. Wonder how he'll do in prison?"

"He's a murderer," Denver said, heading for the

shed to the right of the house. "He's gonna get the rope."

Hendricks looked down at the outlaw, who was still out cold. It was hard to believe he was looking at a living dead man.

# EPILOGUE

Brenda settled back against Hendricks, looking out at their guests. Three months had passed as if time didn't exist. She had never been happier in her life.

"Well, well, well." She looked up at Hendricks, comfortable in her snuggled position against him.

She turned her eyes to see where he was looking and smiled to see Leonard heading toward them. He'd become a good friend in that short amount of time, even buying a small home in Low Branch he said he would use as a recreational cottage whenever he wanted to come by and see his new friends.

True to his word, Leonard had paid for some of the wedding and reception. He introduced them to the pastor of his church, but Brenda insisted they use the pastor from her hometown, who was a friend of her father's.

The wedding ceremony had gone smoothly.

Brenda was now a married woman. Her husband was an ex-bounty hunter. She giggled, thinking about how he'd announced he was taking the deputy position Sheriff Bancroft had offered him. He'd made a huge deal of it, even throwing a dinner party at the boarding house, where there was plenty of room for cooking and socializing. He'd made friends with everyone in town.

"You're not gonna have me chasin' down any more outlaws, right?" Leonard asked, dropping down in a chair opposite the two of them. He laced his fingers together in front of them and gave them a big smile, the left side going up slightly higher than the other side. Something about Leonard Franklin made her feel comfortable. She could tell he had that effect on everyone. It was hard to believe he didn't have a good woman on his arm already.

"Not unless you volunteer for it," was Hendricks's quick response. "Somehow, I don't see that happening. You're pretty happy with your life the way it is, aren't you?"

"That I am, as a matter of fact. I am." He sat back,

his grin getting wider. He reached in his jacket to the inner pocket and pulled out an envelope. He set it on the table and dramatically slid it across to them. "Here is your wedding present. Don't say I never gave you anything."

Brenda giggled, pulling the envelope closer to herself. She glanced at Hendricks, sure that they'd just been provided with the means to live well for years. If there was one thing every person who ever met Leonard knew, he had a lot of money and didn't mind talking about it. He wasn't obnoxious about it, which was probably why he was so beloved.

Then again, many of those people probably had ulterior motives, hoping he would toss some of his wealth their way.

As she had before, Brenda felt sorry for him. She wouldn't wish a lonely life on him.

"Have you found a lady yet?" she asked curiously. "I can't bear to see a good man like you being alone all the time."

"You are concerned for me. How sweet." Leonard smiled. "I will be fine. I'll just write to another lady. Unless you have a sister or a friend, and I think you would have mentioned that to me already if you did."

She nodded at him, tilting her head to the side. "I certainly would have."

Hendricks lifted both hands in the air when the wealthy man turned his eyes to him. "Don't look at me. I don't know any women. That's why I've been single for so long. No sisters either. Maybe you can ask Denver?"

Leonard let out a pleasant laugh. "I'm not desperately looking to fill that position right now. I've got a few projects I've got my hands in. Someone told me to let things come naturally. When I find the right woman, I'll find her."

"Let's hope you don't have to get shot in the side for that to happen," Brenda quipped, glancing at her husband.

Both men laughed. "Well, you open that envelope whenever you like, my friends," Leonard said, pushing himself to his feet, his hands flat on the table in front of him. "I'm gonna go mingle and see if I can find a woman to be on my arm, as you like to put it, Brenda. I'm glad you invited me to your wedding."

"I'm glad we're friends, Leo," Hendricks said, standing. "I didn't mean to take your woman."

Leonard shook his head, letting out a guffaw. "She was never my woman, Hendricks," he said confidently, gesturing with his head. "She was yours before I even showed my face. Glad I did, though. Would have missed out on some good friends. You two take care of each other now. We'll talk again soon."

The couple nodded at him as he merged back into the crowd.

Brenda was quite sure the entire town had shown up for their wedding and after-ceremony party. Even the women Clarice had convinced of Brenda's immorality were there, smiling genuinely at her. One had even spoken to her as if nothing had ever been said behind Brenda's back.

Since they didn't know what she was like before they spoke to Clarice, she didn't hold anything against them. All she wanted was to be friends with the townsfolk of Low Branch since she had decided to stay. Since he didn't have a home of his own, Hendricks was happy to move into the cottage with her and make it his home.

She was aware when Hendricks sat back, putting his arm around her shoulders and massaging her with his large hand. She leaned against him again, resting her head to the side. He was so broad-chested. She couldn't have been more comfortable.

"I love you, Hendricks," she whispered, pressing

herself against him. He squeezed her, lowered his head, and whispered back in her ear. When his breath brushed over her skin, she closed her eyes, enjoying the sensation of tingles that ran down her spine.

"I love you, too. I have since the first time I saw you. I looked at you through your kitchen window when you were out in that garden, and I thought... I thought you were an angel. An angel with long black hair. And then I got to see your eyes. Your amazing, beautiful blue eyes. But you know what the best part of it all was?"

She pulled back slightly so she could look up at him. His smile was warm and loving. She felt his love for her radiating through her when he spoke.

"The best part of it all was when you opened your mouth and spoke. Your appearance is as beautiful as what's inside you. You're strong and resilient. You know what you want, and you go for it. That's how I've always been, too. I loved the fact that you are smart, bold... you're the perfect woman for me."

There was no way for Brenda to express how much she loved him. He'd already taken all the right words. She raised up as high as she could to kiss him. He saw what she was attempting and lowered his head so she wouldn't have to stretch too far.

When their lips met, Brenda felt an explosion inside her. Her heart jumped in her chest, and her blood raced through her veins like fire. She knew at that moment she would be happy for the rest of her life in the arms of her loving husband, the man who had won her heart.

Click here for more Blythe Carver books!

Sign up for the newsletter to be notified of new releases.


Click on link for
Newsletter
or put this in your browser window:


landing.mailerlite.com/webforms/landing/p6l2s1